Patricia Skalka

StarSong

A Novella

LITTLE CREEK PRESS
MINERAL POINT, WISCONSIN

Little Creek Press
5341 Sunny Ridge Road
Mineral Point, WI 53565

Printed in the United States of America

Cataloging-in-Publication Data
Name: Patricia Skalka, author
Title: StarSong: A Novella
Description: Mineral Point, WI Little Creek Press, 2025
Identifiers: LCCN: 2025946216 | ISBN: 978-1-967311-89-7
Classification: FICTION / Death, Grief, Bereavement
FICTION / Family Life / Parenthood & Children
FICTION / Coming of Age

Book design by Little Creek Press

Human Authored,™ Reg #: 7476715, https://authorsguild.org/human

For Julia and Carla,
who each asked the question . . .

PRAISE FOR *STARSONG*

"Here's a finely tuned story about the power of belief and the miraculous force of a daughter's love. Skalka's clean prose moves the plot forward at a gratifying pace."

—John Mauk, host of Prose from the Underground, a free video series

"*StarSong* builds like a symphony. Relationships are the melody while exterior forces provide the percussion and the extranatural builds a secondary theme, until the climax brings everything together in a true ode to joy. Fans of Skalka's Dave Cubiak series will instantly recognize her trademark graceful prose and ability to balance strength and trauma with humanity's place in the natural world. In this case, the mystery to be solved isn't a murder but one of both heart and heartbreak. An absorptive read and a plot that pulls you along because you must reach that satisfying and beautiful conclusion. I loved it and was sad to leave Georgia's world. As ever, Skalka is a Must Read and *StarSong* is yet another reason Skalka has earned her place as one of the Midwest's most notable and readable authors."

—Wendy Wimmer, *Entry Level*, Kirkus Reviews Best Indie Short Fiction

"*StarSong* is the lovely story of a young girl whose violin answers loss with a call to heaven . . . enchanting."

—Mary Logue, Dreki: *My Icelandic Dragon*

“A story about a child’s love for her mother, the pain of loss, the forces that hold families together, and the complexities of reason and faith. Patricia Skalka’s moving, fable-like story is intimate in its depiction of a family in turmoil, and vast in its vision of a redemptive, ultimately benevolent universe. These characters, drawn with such care and sensitivity, will stay with me. *StarSong* is a little gem.”

—Kevin Prufer, author of *Sleepaway*

“A beautiful meditation on love, loss, and coming of age, shot through with music. When a seat on a changed flight takes a young girl's mother in a fiery crash, life is hardest for those left behind. But death is not entirely what we believe it to be, as Patricia Skalka ponders in this lovely, resonant novella, which, like life, seems all too fleeting.”

—Jenny Milchman, *USA Today* bestselling (Mary Higgins Clark award winning) author of The Fairest in the Arles Shepherd series

PART ONE

Love

The year that I turned ten, autumn rolled down from the Great Smoky Mountains in quick, spectacular fashion. Overnight the giant Shumard oak outside my bedroom turned flaming red, just in time for my birthday. Across the region, local farmers boasted of oversized pumpkins and swore that the sorghum molasses was the sweetest corn syrup ever produced. Winter, too, arrived majestically, bearing a gift of snow, a welcome and rare treat in our part of the country.

Others may remember that year for these natural phenomena, but I remember those precious few months for the unbearable grief that they brought and for the joy that followed. I remember the year because of what happened on the stubby hill behind our white clapboard house on Christmas Eve.

I am an old woman now, but those events are seared into my memory. Despite the decades that have dulled my vision, I see them as clearly as I spied the scarlet tree when I woke up and looked out the window that late September morning.

Our house was at the end of South Granite Street. My father, Harry Weldon, was a professor of anatomy at the local college. He was a large, gruff man whose students addressed him as "doctor." My mother, Sherry Weldon, was also a doctor, but a different kind. Dr. Sherry Weldon was a pediatric surgeon at the local hospital, and she was as soft-spoken and gentle as my father was loud and stern. They often disagreed about unimportant things, like when to prune the crab apple tree out front, and on important issues as well, like how to raise a child and what values to impart to me, their daughter, Georgia. My mother was a believer; my father was not.

A rambling porch wrapped around the front of the house, and in the rear, a screened sunroom opened to an orange brick patio and a deep backyard that was home to the giant oak. The tree was too large for me to climb, so my father built a platform in the lower branches and nailed four boards to the trunk, making it easy for me to access my perch. From there, I'd look out toward the grassy field that lay behind our yard and the neighbors' yards as well. Beyond the flat meadow, the ground gently sloped upward and bubbled into a hill. Not a summit like one of the foothills that loomed in the distance, but a steep enough rise that racing to the top left me winded. Over time, our house changed with each subsequent owner. There's even a new wing, and both the patio and the venerable oak are gone. I'd like to think the tree died of old age, but I don't know. Only the hill looks much the same, but now I'm too arthritic to climb to the summit. Now I can only look up and remember.

For my birthday that year, we hung paper lanterns and a piñata from the oak. If I could go back, I would stop time at the moment I swung the bat at the papier-mâché donkey that dangled from the lowest branch. I missed the target because I was watching my parents smile at each other, and I remember thinking that I had never seen them so happy.

Two days later, at seven o'clock in the morning, my mother knocked on my door. She tapped twice. This was her special code: two taps, two hugs, two kisses. The first meant *love*. The second meant *you*.

Her brown hair was pulled back into a low bun, and, as usual, she was fully dressed, because surgeries were scheduled first thing in the day, and she had to be at the hospital early. Normally, she'd leave after I was up, and my hour before school was spent with my father. But that morning, the first day of October, was special because my mother was driving me to school for show-and-tell.

There were twenty-three of us in the fifth grade at Spencer Elementary School, and each of us was encouraged to invite a guest to talk about their hobbies or jobs. I hadn't asked my father because we all knew what a teacher did. But a doctor? Or more precisely, a surgeon? I was sure my mother would be a hit. As we pulled into the parking lot, however, I began to fret. The only time I'd ever been really ill with a bad sore throat, my parents took me to a doctor who talked to me like I was a baby. Would my mother do that? I was mortified at the thought of it.

We were out of the car and crunching across the gravel parking lot before I noticed the large yellow envelope in her left hand. People said that my mother had the hands of a surgeon. When I was younger, I thought it meant "smart hands," but by then I was old enough to know that the words meant that she had steady, agile hands. Hands that were guided by a steady, agile mind.

"What's that?" I said, trying to swallow the panic in my voice.

"Oh, just something I thought your classmates would be interested in," she said.

"Nutrition charts?"

My mother laughed. "You'll see."

Ahead of us, the three-story red brick school loomed over the playground. As we passed through the sea of children in their blue and white uniforms, I glanced around, wary of seeing anyone I knew. "What are you going to talk about?" I asked.

"Doctor stuff."

Good health habits, I thought, and groaned inwardly. My mother was going to be a bore, and I would be embarrassed forever.

When we reached the stairs, I hesitated.

"What's wrong, Georgia?"

"Nothing."

"Come on," my mother said, setting her foot on the first step.

Then, she repeated my name, using her are-you-okay-or-is-there-something-you-want-to-tell-me voice.

I swallowed and slid my foot next to hers. We climbed the stairs together and opened the heavy door to the familiar green corridor. The wide hall was hushed, save for the sporadic click of a distant typewriter, and the air was lightly spiced with the aroma of floor polish. Photos of the first graduation classes lined the wall near the entrance. As we moved past the pictures, our faces were reflected off the glass and blurred with the images of the students poised on the front lawn, fragmenting us into a series of collages. Just pieces. A little of me. A little of my mother. A little of smiling children I'd never met.

Hurrying alongside my mother, I felt my spirits lift and my doubts evaporate. By the time we were halfway down the corridor, I was eager for her presentation and oblivious to the unseen twin paths of disaster and miracle that stretched before us.

My teacher was waiting outside Room 104. That day Miss Elizabeth Graham had added a strand of pearls to her uniform slim skirt and pastel sweater set, and I was sure she'd done so out of deference to my mother.

Where I grew up, women usually nodded politely to each other when they were introduced. But that morning, Miss Graham, who was barely as tall as the shortest eighth-grade boy, surprised me by extending her hand to my mother.

"We are privileged to have you here," she said. She blushed

slightly as she spoke, and the pink in her cheeks made her smoky gray eyes seem mysterious and deep. “Thank you for taking time from your very busy schedule,” she continued. “I know the children will be thrilled.” Miss Graham was from Alabama and said “y’all” when she addressed the class and “fixin’ to” when she was about to do something. Her greeting to my mother was delivered with the kind of soft Southern accent that even in our region registered as different.

My mother smiled and shook Miss Graham’s hand. “It’s an honor,” she said, sounding slightly Southern herself for a moment.

In the classroom, I took my seat near the front while my mother waited in the rear. Although show-and-tell was first on the morning schedule, the normal business of the school day still had to be dispensed with beforehand. I fidgeted through the PA announcements about the fall raffle and tryouts for the school play. With my classmates, I stood and recited the Pledge of Allegiance. Then I sat back down while Miss Graham took attendance and collected the lunch milk money.

Finally, the routine tasks were completed, and my teacher gave me the nod. Because my mother was my guest, I had both the responsibility and the honor of introducing her.

As I pried myself loose from the chair, I realized that I hadn’t prepared anything to say. I had envisioned myself being brilliant and amusing, the way Ed Sullivan was when he welcomed his guests to the stage.

But I wasn’t.

“This is Doctor Sherry Weldon,” I said, pouring all the pride I could into the words. Then I ruined it. "She's my mom." The words came out like a bleat, and everyone laughed. My face turned red, and I slid into my seat. Earlier, I'd worried about my mother embarrassing me, and here I'd done that to her.

Apparently, she didn't notice. For the next half hour, pediatric surgeon Dr. Sherry Weldon wowed my classmates. I'd never thought of my mother as a show-woman, but there she was, telling funny stories from medical school and sharing tales of operating room heroics as she paced back and forth in front of the class.

I was so enthralled listening to her that I'd forgotten about the large yellow envelope until she picked it up off the desk. I held my breath.

"I have something very special here," she said.

There wasn't a sound in the room.

With a flourish, my mother pulled out three sheets of X-ray film. The pieces were big and heavy, like thick see-through plastic. The first was an image of the human chest. This really got the students' attention.

"Dense tissue such as bone shows up white," she said, pointing to a long column that ran from the top of the picture to the bottom. "Can anyone tell me what this is?"

Five hands shot into the air.

"The spine!" several voices called out together.

"Yes, and these are the ribs." My mother ran a finger along two of the delicate bones that curved into an open cage. "And these are the lungs." She tapped the two black smudges that resembled toed-in footprints.

Ugh. The class recoiled.

"You're probably thinking that the patient was a heavy smoker and that's why his lungs appear black, but that's not true."

We looked at each other, puzzled.

"When X-rays pass through what is mostly air, the image shows up black. That means that these are the lungs of a healthy person. The lungs of a smoker are filled with particles and sometimes cancer, which show up as white blobs. The more white splotches there are in the lungs, the less air the person can inhale."

My mother's gaze swept over the class. "And the lesson is?"

"Don't smoke," we sang out together.

"Excellent." She put down the lung X-ray and held up the second image.

"Here's a fracture in the wrist of a six-year-old girl," she said, indicating the thin seam in the bone. "And this," she said, lifting the third, "is a fracture in the foot of a ten-year-old boy."

The X-rays were passed from one child to another, as my mother explained how broken bones were set and how they mended.

"Now for a quiz. How many bones are in the body of an average child?"

I knew the answer but thought it unfair to respond. So I kept my hand down.

"Ninety-four," someone in the last row called out.

"More than that. The body of the average child contains more than two hundred bones."

The class fell silent, as if absorbing this astonishing fact.

"And how many quarts of blood?"

This time there were no wild guesses proffered.

I knew the answer to this question, too, but didn't volunteer a response for fear of looking like a smarty pants.

"Each of you has between two and three quarts of blood flowing in your veins," my mother told the class.

Toby Peters raised her hand. Toby had freckles and bouncy red hair. She was my best friend and next-door neighbor. "If you have an accident and lose half of your blood, will you die?" she asked.

"That's an excellent question, Toby," my mother said. "If a child loses that much blood, then unfortunately, yes, he or she will die. But there's very little chance of that happening to any of you. We have good hospitals, and we know so very much about treating trauma patients. And, if needed, we can give lifesaving blood to patients through transfusions."

Just then, a bell rang in the hall.

I hadn't noticed Miss Graham move from her spot, but suddenly she was up front, next to my mother. "Children, do we have something to say to our visitor?" she said.

On cue, my classmates and I bellowed a singsong "Thank you, Doctor Weldon" to our day's guest speaker.

I was pleased when Miss Graham gave me permission to accompany my mother to the front door. Although she'd been to the school for teacher conferences and holiday programs and didn't need help finding her way, a student escort was a courtesy afforded every guest, and she was no exception.

"How'd I do?" my mother asked as soon as we were in the hall.

You were marvelous, I wanted to tell her, but before I could answer, the door to the music room swung open and Ludwig Maier emerged. Shoulders slumped and head down, the gray-haired maestro advanced toward us.

"Ah, two of my favorite ladies," he said as he stepped into our path and bowed deeply.

At this, I made a silly, giggly noise which neither of them seemed to notice.

Mr. Maier had once been a man of average height, but age had bent his back and collapsed his vertebrae several inches. He extended his hand, and my mother stooped to accommodate his shriveled frame. With my father, she often joked that she survived in the male-dominated hospital only on account of her physical presence. At nearly six feet tall, she towered over a good number of the other physicians, and those she didn't surpass in stature, she met eye to eye. "They can't ignore me," she said. "I won't let them."

When she said this to my father, her demeanor was always strong and defiant. But with Mr. Maier, her manner was soft and kind.

"Sir, it is an honor," she said and clasped his hand.

At home, my parents used the words *genius* and *treasure* to describe Ludwig Maier.

"The man could be conducting at Carnegie Hall," my father said.

"You have no idea how lucky you are to have him at your school," my mother added.

"But he's so odd," I said. "Sometimes he wears different colored socks!"

My mother laughed. "Odd is not bad, and if you know what's good for you, you'll ignore his eccentricities and learn all you can from him."

A music professor of note, Mr. Maier had taught for years at a small, prestigious college in a neighboring town. Forced out by age and jealous rivals, he refused to walk away from his profession and took a part-time job as a music teacher at Spencer Elementary. Within weeks, he formed a school orchestra, welcoming even the youngest to play.

I was in the first grade when the maestro was hired, and initially I feared the hunched, somber man with the thundering voice. I wasn't alone. No one I knew wanted to be in his class, and we all resisted the repeated invitations to sign up for orchestra. Then halfway through the school year Toby joined, and what Toby did, I did too.

Toby was a klutz. That's not being mean, just honest. She tripped whenever she tried to run. At least three times a week, she knocked over her carton of milk at lunch. When she tied her shoes, the laces on one foot raced to become undone before those on the other.

"I don't know what we're going to do with you," I once heard her mother tell her.

When Toby picked up the violin, her awkwardness disappeared.

It was as if the instrument filled a missing space and made her whole. She understood the violin in a way that the rest of us could not comprehend. Everyone wanted to be able to play like Toby.

Before long, the rehearsal room was filled with young, fledgling musicians. To our wonder and delight, the old maestro possessed a bottomless supply of patience and unwavering faith in our abilities. Those first few weeks, the screeches that we drew forth from our miniature stringed instruments must have been torture to his ears, but he never complained.

"Good, good. And it will get better," he said.

I didn't believe him. But I soon learned that I was wrong. Little by little, we began to produce sounds that approximated music. Mr. Maier was delighted. "Even the greatest started at the beginning," he'd remind us. As he coaxed us along, the maestro created a mystical link between the music and the instruments that propelled us to plateaus high above our individual abilities. By the time my mother and I met him in the hall that day, all this was history. I'd become devoted to him and to the violin and had advanced from beginner to intermediate orchestra.

"Georgia's nervous but also very excited about the fall concert," my mother told Mr. Maier.

Of course, I was. The fall concert was a euphemism for the upcoming state competition. Mr. Maier encouraged us to think of it as just another performance, but we all knew it was more than that. We'd travel by bus to another city and compete against school orchestras from across the state, many of them far more established than ours. Who wouldn't be nervous and excited?

Mr. Maier patted my mother's hand. "Good, good, *mein Liebchen*. She will do well," he said.

At this, he glanced at me, and I felt my face redden.

"You will attend, of course," he said, turning back to my mother.

"Mr. Weldon and I will both be there. We wouldn't miss it for the world," she said.

"Good, good," he said again. Then he bowed once more and went on his way.

At the exit, I shouldered the door open, kissed my mother on the cheek, and said goodbye. With the sun warm on my face, I watched her descend the stairs and retrace our earlier path. When she reached the sidewalk, I turned and hurried back to my classroom. Running was not allowed in the halls, so I went past the office at the speediest walk I could manage. The moment I was out of sight, I broke into a trot, and by the time I was fifty feet from the door to Room 104, I was in a full-blown sprint.

My desk was near the front, in the row farthest from the door and nearest the wall of windows that overlooked the grounds. I got to my seat just as my mother reached her car. I waved and she waved back. Then she opened the door and slipped behind the wheel.

"Georgia," Miss Graham said, indicating that I was to take my seat.

Pretending I hadn't heard, I grabbed a notebook off the corner of my desk and flipped through the pages. As I did so, I glanced outside just in time to see my mother flash the headlights on her car. Once. Twice. I grinned. That's what I'd been waiting for. What

I had been in such a hurry to witness.

The lights flashed again.

"Love you, too," I whispered and sat down.

We had orchestra practice after school that afternoon, and by the time I got home, it was five. I was surprised to find my mother in the kitchen preparing dinner. Although she was a good cook, she rarely left the hospital early enough to do more than boil water for pasta. That evening's meal took on the appearance of a full-blown Sunday dinner. Small, red-skinned potatoes simmered on the stove, and the wonderful aroma of garlic-rubbed roast chicken filled the room.

I ate half an apple and then sat at the kitchen table and started to write my report on *Tuck Everlasting*, a novel about a family that becomes immortal after drinking from a secret spring. I was on the second page when I remembered my mother's presentation to my class that morning.

"What happens when you die?" I asked.

She turned from the counter where she'd been chopping parsley for the potatoes. "What do you mean?"

"At school today you said that a kid, someone like me or one of my friends, would die if they lost half their blood."

My mother eyed me closely. "Yes, under extreme circumstances that could happen. If you lose enough blood, your heart stops beating and you die," she said.

"Does dying hurt?"

"Sometimes it does. But not always."

"Do people know they're dying?"

My mother set the knife down and scooped the parsley into a small bowl.

"That's not an easy question to answer," she said, swiping her hands on her checkered apron. "For some people, death comes without warning."

"Like in an accident?"

"Yes. Like that. And other times people become very ill and are able to anticipate death."

In retrospect, I realize that some people would find this kind of candid back-and-forth between a mother and her ten-year-old daughter uncomfortable. But as a parent, my mother believed in being honest about life. And as a doctor, she knew the answers to my questions, so how could she not respond as she did?

"Do you think they're scared? The people who can anticipate dying?"

My mother opened a cabinet and took out three plates. "I think that some might be because they don't know what to expect," she said as she set the dishes on the counter. "For those who believe in life after death, it might be a different experience."

"Do you think people are aware of leaving their bodies and going to another place?"

At the stove again, my mother lifted the lid from the potatoes and made a show of testing one with a fork. I think she was stalling for time. "I don't know. No one does, because no one has ever returned to tell anyone about it," she said and put the lid back in place. "Houdini supposedly tried. You know who he is, don't you?"

"The man who escaped from locked trunks."

"Well, yes, he did that and more. He promised his wife that after he died, he would contact her if he could. They came up with a secret code he was supposed to use, so she'd know it was him."

"Did it work?"

"There were some stories that claimed he had, and others that said it was a hoax. So it's never been proven."

"Will you? Try, I mean?"

She tousled my short hair and laughed, but it was a kind laugh. "Hopefully the occasion won't arise for many years, but for you, anything."

I refused to be put off lightly. "Will you?" I said again, urgent and insistent.

Something in my tone made my mother pause. In the redolent kitchen, she gazed out the window. She was quiet for so long that I began to get nervous. Had I been wrong to ask again after she said she would?

Finally, she turned back to me. "I believe that there is some form of life after death, and so, yes, if it is possible, I will do it. If it is impossible, I will at least try," she said.

"Promise?"

"Promise."

At that moment, the rear door swung open, and my father strode into the kitchen. “Promises. Promises. Sounds like you’re composing a TV commercial for a new perfume,” he said. His glasses fogged up immediately. He pulled them off with one hand and doffed his newsboy cap with the other.

Then he gave my mother a quick hug, kissed my forehead, and walked toward the stove.

“Don’t . . . ,” my mother said. Too late, the oven door was open.

My father leaned down and inhaled deeply.

“Pure ambrosia,” he declared, as he straightened up. “Who needs perfume? You could bottle the aroma and put us all on easy street.”

We ate dinner at six. All my friends had formal dining rooms, but ours was very simple. We had a plain pine table and straight-back chairs. There was no china and crystal stemware in the corner hutch or on the shelves that stood from floor to ceiling. Only books. And instead of lace curtains, the windows were decorated with hanging plants. The room faced east, and until noon, it caught the sun; by dinnertime it was in shadow. The only light came from four dim ceiling bulbs, one in each corner of the overhead beams, and the glow of two flickering candles set at opposite ends of the table. The view through the green jungle was similarly layered in dark and light. The top of the hill and the clouds above were lit by the rays of the setting sun that skimmed over the treetops from the west. But the slope and the field at the base were dark, almost foreboding.

We'd moved on to dessert when my father abruptly looked up from his bowl of apple crisp and fixed his eyes on my mother, who sat across from him. "I heard what you were talking about earlier, when I got home." There was no joviality in his voice, and sensing what was to come, I put down my spoon.

"Maybe it's just my natural cynicism, but I don't think you should be filling Georgia with such ideas. You are merely duping her, postponing the inevitable grasp of truth. And you," he said, brightening and good-naturedly waving his spoon at me, "shouldn't be so gullible."

I nodded because I knew what he meant. My mother and I both did. The concepts of eternity and life after death were subjects about which my parents disagreed, so this was a familiar point of contention between them.

I lived in a house divided. My mother was a believer. My father was not. My mother prayed. He didn't.

Sitting at the table, the dregs of our dinner spread before us, he went on. "Since you've had your say, now is the time for me to have mine." He pivoted toward the end of the table where I sat. "We live. We die. Life ends. That's my perspective, for what it's worth. I know it sounds harsh, especially to your young ears, but that's what I believe. Okay?"

Before I could respond—not that I knew what I would say—my mother intervened.

"I was simply expressing my opinion, to which you would agree that I am entitled," she said. "Georgia will make up her own mind in due time. And you, my dear," she said, as she reached over and took my father's hand, "if you live long enough, will have a change of heart as well."

My father harrumphed.

My mother smiled. "Science and logic can't explain everything," she said.

My father harrumphed again.

Later when I was finishing my homework, my father knocked on my door. I thought he was going to continue his dinner lecture, but he'd already moved on. "A perfect night for star gazing," he said.

"It's cold out," I said and shuddered in protest.

"Bundle up. You'll be fine. Your mother's waiting for us downstairs."

Five minutes later, the three of us were in the yard and heading toward the hill. I was right. It was cold. The temperature had dipped low enough that I could see a wisp of my own breath each time I exhaled. But wearing a hat and gloves as well as my winter jacket, I felt almost as cozy as I had in my room.

Truthfully, I enjoyed our evening forays. There was something a little scary about the hill in the dark, and it seemed special that the three of us were willing to take it on together. As we climbed away from the streetlights and the brightly lit houses, the darkness intensified. Trying not to imagine monsters lurking in the shadows, I led the way, training my yellow flashlight on one of the paths that Toby and I had beaten down over the summer months. The solitary beam proved a feeble defense against the dark cloak that enveloped us, but I knew the way and walked quickly. My father followed with the telescope and my mother with a thermos of hot chocolate.

That night an unusual number of stars were visible, and I craned my neck to take them all in. There was one odd exception. No matter how clear it was and how many celestial forms shone and sparkled overhead, a small patch of sky just above the northwest horizon remained stubbornly dark.

"It's like a piece of prime real estate waiting for new stars to move in," my father once said.

Of course, we were on the hill for a reason. The first was to view the rings of Saturn, which were normally not visible in our part of the country. The second became evident after we'd each taken a turn at the telescope and were sipping cups of hot chocolate.

"There are far reaches of the universe that we can't even imagine. Planets, other solar systems, things we can barely conceive of. The latest theory," my father said, raising his arm and then moving it from left to right, "is that the cosmos may be filled with invisible magnetic waves, forces that we don't know how to capture and decipher." He fell quiet for a moment. "If there is life out there, evidence will be borne not in myth but on the mysterious waves that even now are invading Earth's atmosphere."

My mother smiled at his pronouncement. "Anything is possible," she said.

On Saturday, my parents hosted their annual fall party. During the afternoon my father made his famous chili while Toby and I helped my mother with the rest of the preparations.

We were the first to taste the chili. Spicy!

The first to sample the cheeses. Stinky!

The first to try my mother's homemade French bread. Perfect.

I felt like Goldilocks.

In the evening, as the guests began to arrive, Toby and I were upstairs trying to translate The Beatles' "I Saw Her Standing There" into French. We got as far as "*Eh bien, elle avait juste dix-sept ans*" when we decided to check out the party.

Crouched at the top of the stairs, we peered between the banister spindles. We couldn't make out what anyone said—the noise that drifted up the stairwell was a drone of voices interspersed with the occasional laugh—but we liked looking at these folks. Usually, we saw them either in their work apparel or the casual clothes they wore on Saturdays while doing chores. Tonight they seemed different, sophisticated in their sport coats and fancy dresses, with drinks in one hand and many with cigarettes in the other. Most of the people were familiar: doctors from the hospital; professors from the college, including Toby's mathematician father, Peter P. Peters, the tallest man in the room and the only one with a mustache; Mrs. Peters with her blonde braids regally wrapped around her head; and neighbors from up and down the street.

"What do you think they're talking about?" Toby asked.

"Office politics," I said, trying to sound as if I knew what that meant.

Someone must have told a joke because they were all laughing.

In the din, the doorbell rang. I was about to run down when my mother stepped into the hall and opened the door to Ludwig Maier.

The maestro was still bent at the shoulders, but somehow he seemed younger. His mop of hair was combed, and he wore a suit that looked newer than the one he wore at school.

"My dear," he said, handing my mother a bouquet of yellow roses. She kissed his cheek and then took his elbow and walked him into the gathering.

I was surprised to see our music teacher at the party. I was even more surprised to realize that everyone seemed to know him. Head bobbing, he slowly sifted through the clusters of guests. The men shook his hand, and the women gave him quick hugs or bussed his cheek.

"I didn't know Mr. Maier was so popular," I whispered to Toby.

"Of course he's popular. He's famous," she said.

"Oh, right."

Impressed with Toby's reasoning and annoyed that I hadn't figured out as much, I turned to study my parents.

Like Mr. Maier, my father also seemed younger. He'd been pretty animated through the afternoon and hadn't slowed down at all. If anything, he was talking more than usual. Once or twice I picked out his rich baritone followed by a burst of laughter. *Cool,*

Dad, I thought as he and two other men made their way to the kitchen.

My mother remained in the living room with a cluster of women. They all wore nice dresses, but hers was different. Baubles and ruffles were big that season, and in a gathering filled with gaudy jewelry and frills in bright pinks, blues, and yellows, there was my mom in a plain, forest green sheath and a strand of pearls.

"Your mom is so groovy," Toby said. "I'll bet she doesn't iron your shoelaces."

I looked at my friend aghast. "Your mother irons your shoelaces?"

"Yeah."

"That's weird. When I grow up, I'm not even going to own an iron. I think they're stupid."

Toby agreed.

We started to list all the other things that as adults we wouldn't own or do, when a loud thumping noise from the first floor drew our attention back to the party.

Below us, the sofa and chairs were being pushed aside, the lights dimmed, and the volume on the stereo cranked up.

"Oh, my gosh, they're dancing," I said as the gyrating mass of sensible adults we knew as our parents and teachers did the twist.

Toby and I laughed out loud, but no one downstairs noticed. They were too busy tossing their bodies one way and then the other, desperately trying to stay on top of the beat. Even Mr. Maier was dancing! And when Toby's mother started twirling her hand in the air, we nearly collapsed in a fit of hysterics.

I've been on this earth for many decades, and I still think that one of the most wonderful absurdities about life is that people are capable of dancing without having any idea of how silly they look. No one at the party was going to be inhibited by the fact that they didn't know what they were doing. Even my parents looked ridiculous, but oh so happy.

Before long, Toby and I were on our feet, *twisting* in the upstairs hall. We did the jitterbug, too, and stumbled along to a cha-cha, but after a while we got bored and went to my room.

Toby was staying overnight, so my mother had left an extra blanket and a second pillow on the bed. Using books as weights, we anchored the blue and white checkered blanket to the desk and then draped it over the chair. Lying side by side inside our makeshift tent, we pulled the other covers up to our chins and read. We'd planned to stay awake until midnight, but I don't think we made it that late. I didn't hear anyone leave, but the next morning, when the sun woke us up, the house was empty and quiet. Once downstairs, we made ourselves toast for breakfast, and then Toby went home.

For lunch my mom heated the leftover chili, and afterward we drove into the country to buy apples and pumpkins. Half of the apples were reserved for eating, and half were for pies. The pumpkins were for display. We put one out front and three on the patio. Closer to Halloween, we'd carve faces into them and line them up on the front porch, lit with candles.

I was on my way upstairs to read when my father stopped me.

"Time for practice," he said.

Usually, I practiced violin every day for thirty minutes, but on Saturday I'd been given a pass because of the party. That meant I had to play for a full hour. I started to protest but then realized that Toby had probably been practicing all afternoon, and I knew if I ever wanted to be half as good as she was, I had work to do.

One day the previous spring, Ludwig Maier had sailed into orchestra rehearsal with more than his usual enthusiasm.

"I will play for you something magnificent," he said, as he eased a record album from its jacket and then carefully set the platter on the turntable. "From Mr. Ludwig van Beethoven. The final movement from his *Ninth Symphony*," he announced. The school day was over, and with the building largely empty of both students and teachers, he turned the volume up high. The music began with a simple melody that circled around on itself as it innocently billowed in intensity and then magically erupted into an explosion of sound so eloquent and overwhelming that I clamped my hands over my ears.

"No," the old instructor said. "Listen! Feel!"

Reluctantly, I lowered my hands to my lap and let the music sweep over me as he played the movement a second time.

In the silence that followed, Mr. Maier announced that we would perform the "Ode to Joy" at the fall concert.

I blinked back tears. "I can't play that," I said. "It's much too grand."

The other students nodded in agreement, and our beloved

teacher looked on with dismay. Then he popped his hand against the side of his head and laughed. "Of course, you will not play *that*. That was a performance by the Chicago Symphony Orchestra, and, good as you are, you are not the CSO. No, you will play the movement written for a student orchestra, without the chorus. Still beautiful. Like this."

He put another record on the turntable and played a simplified version of the movement.

When it finished, Mr. Maier knelt by me and took my hands in his. "This you can do," he said. Knees creaking, he stood and extended his arms to the group. "This you all can do."

And you know what happened? We stood and cheered because we believed him.

"This music was Beethoven's most magnificent prayer, and as with all prayers, it came from his heart. If you play from the heart"—Mr. Maier pressed his fist to his chest and pulled us in with his steadfast gaze—"all of the universe will hear you."

We cheered again.

The maestro held up his hand. "Ah, but first you must learn. Then you must practice. And when you think you are the best, you will know that you have begun crawling toward your goal, and you will start all over."

We groaned, but we were happy. Mr. Maier had broken the tension and allayed our fears. As we began our foray into the world of Beethoven, the simplicity of the opening notes drew us along. After being overwhelmed listening to the piece, I remember thinking how easy it seemed once I started playing it. Four-four time. B-B-C-D-D-C-B-A-G-G-A-B-B-A-A. One beat per note except for the last, then repeat the sequence.

At home that afternoon, my face still rosy from our outing, I played the movement all the way through while my father sat in his favorite chair and listened.

"The 'Ode to Joy.' A very lovely piece," he said.

"It's the greatest prayer," I said, quoting Mr. Maier.

"It's the greatest music," my father replied sanguinely.

About halfway through the session, my mother came and joined him. Playing for my parents made me feel important and confident. *I love this music*, I thought. *I want to play it forever.*

The weekend ended with my father making martinis for my mom and himself, and the three of us gathering around the dining room table for our traditional Sunday evening Scrabble game. When my parents first invited me to join them, I was allowed to misspell words and even make up my own, as long as I could define them. Now I had to use real words and spell them correctly. I was permitted to use the dictionary—the only privilege accorded me. Even then, I never won. I never even came close, but I didn't mind. I delighted in the lighthearted banter between my parents as they challenged each other's entries. I was comforted by the sense of belonging that came from feeling part of this unit, this family.

There would never be another Scrabble game for the three of us, another evening like this. Life in our house on South Granite Street was beautifully ordinary, and it was all about to change.

PART TWO

Loss

The next day, on a morning shot through with October's magic light, my mother packed a cheese sandwich and an apple for my lunch and prepared a special French toast breakfast for me. I was still eating when a blue taxi pulled up in front of the house to take her to the airport, where she would board a plane and fly to a medical convention in Miami.

"I'll only be gone for three days," she said the evening before when she kissed me goodnight. "Home before you know it."

It was a short trip, but an important one. My mother, Dr. Sherry Weldon, was to preside over a session on emergency treatment for pediatric trauma patients. Crammed into her worn leather satchel was the report she would present, describing the treatment method she had developed to increase survival rates among accident victims with primary ecchymosis hemorrhage. I didn't understand the medical terminology, but I knew from what she had told me and my father that the technique could prevent children from dying because of severe blood loss. And I knew that was a good thing.

Many of the physicians attending the convention were trauma specialists, and my mother was offering them an effective, minimally invasive procedure to stop hemorrhagic flow and prevent hypovolemic shock following serious injury. Earlier, after she'd finished her report, my mom had positioned herself at the far end of the living room and presented her findings to an audience of two: my father and me.

"The technique is far more effective than the traditional tourniquets used to stem severe, life-threatening blood loss," she said. "A tourniquet may prove lifesaving in the very short term, but it can cause irreparable harm to healthy tissue if left in place too long."

Beyond that, I didn't understand much, but when I was older, I would learn that my mother had developed a technique for splicing and suturing that allowed for the quick, temporary joining of the tunica adventitia, the outer arterial wall. Her approach resulted in minimal blood loss and ensured continued blood flow to healthy tissue and limbs until more permanent repairs could be made. Since the beginning of the year, emergency room doctors at several area hospitals had used the technique and reported their results to my mother.

Standing before us, she held up a chart that documented the data from the nine-month trial. "This will be projected on the wall behind me during my talk," she said, turning as if to point to the image.

"Both immediate and long-term prognosis of every patient treated with the new technique was excellent." Although the procedure was far from proven, she hoped other physicians would agree to use the approach in their emergency rooms, perhaps even teaching it to the paramedics with whom they worked.

"With enough data, we can either prove or disprove the usefulness of the concept. If the initial findings are substantiated, we will be able to present the medical profession with a technique that saves time, money, and lives."

Our two-person audience erupted in applause.

All that Tuesday morning, I imagined my mother on her trip. Taking her seat on the plane, clicking her seatbelt, looking out the window, and watching the ground drop away during takeoff. Once she was airborne, I imagined her sitting back and reviewing her notes, and then, after landing, taking another taxi to the hotel. She'd shown me the brochure of where she was staying. The hotel was right on the beach! Even then, it had a huge swimming pool.

"Don't forget to pack your bathing suit," I said.

"Oh, Georgia, there won't be time for swimming."

Then why have a conference in Miami? I wondered.

Anyway, I imagined my mother floating in the pool and then later having dinner with her colleagues. I liked that word, and my mom must have as well because she used it a lot. "My colleagues," she'd say. "All those men."

On Wednesday morning, I pictured my mother giving her talk. She was slated for ten o'clock, and as I sat in geography class, I imagined her at the podium, the graph projected behind her on the wall. In my perfect-world daydream, I imagined a large room full of her colleagues eagerly leaning forward to catch every word and then peppering her with questions, perhaps even offering a bit of what my mother called constructive criticism. And, of course, thunderous applause at the end.

But that's not what happened.

That evening my mother called while my dad and I were devouring sausage pizza at the kitchen table, and I was sitting close enough to the phone to hear everything she said. Her voice was loud and angry.

"They couldn't wait until I finished to flee from the room. Their damn egos wouldn't allow them to hear anything new—certainly not from a woman," she said.

My father immediately rose to her defense.

"They're a bunch of nitwit prima donnas and blind idiots. Don't pay them any mind. You don't need them. You can gather and substantiate the data yourself. It will just take longer."

My mother continued fretting, but as they talked, she gradually calmed down, and eventually she acquiesced. It was true, she said, she could do the necessary work herself.

"You're right. I'll show them yet," she told my father.

When he hung up, he turned to me. "You heard all that?"

I grimaced. "Yes."

"I'm sorry those other doctors were so blindly rude, but life's not always fair. Remember this, though: Your mother never gives up, and she always does what's right."

The next morning, my mother checked out of the hotel and caught an early flight home. We didn't know about this change of plans until later. We didn't know anything until later. My father fed me the details in bits, as he thought I could handle them. It took years for me to fully understand everything that transpired on that awful day.

My mother was the third connecting passenger on the DC-10, which was en route from the Bahamas to Knoxville. At 10:03 a.m., the wide-body jet pulled away from the gate at Miami International Airport. The aircraft was fully loaded with 290 passengers, seven flight attendants, and a three-member flight crew that included a captain with over twenty years experience flying commercial jets. Under a bright blue sky, the plane taxied down the south runway. Then the pilot made a smooth turn to the right, slowed, and pivoted again to the right before rolling to a stop. They were fourth in line. At precisely 10:18, they received the signal that it was their turn to take off. The cabin lights dimmed, the three engines kicked in, and the 120-ton aircraft lumbered forward. On this flight, my mother had an aisle seat, but as the plane's wheels lifted off the pavement, she would have leaned forward to look past her seatmate toward the window.

The plane quickly climbed to ten thousand feet and was nearly two miles above the ground, when a black crack emerged in the left wing. In rapid, almost simultaneous succession, the rupture snaked down the length of the wing to the pylon, the structural component that held the engine in place. As the pylon broke free, the massive aircraft shuddered and lurched to the side.

Seconds later, in the type of scenario that was never supposed to happen, the engine fell off, releasing a gush of wine-colored hydraulic fluid and forcing the plane to tilt even further. The jet rolled until it was perpendicular to the ground. Imitating the kind of terrifying ride a modern Dante might create for an amusement park from hell, the aircraft plummeted downward. In the tower, the air traffic controllers listened as the captain and flight crew struggled to right the crippled plane.

Then the two remaining engines shut down.

Outside the steel coffin, the atmosphere grew eerily still. Inside, I imagine that my mother called out for my father and for me, while around her, the passengers screamed in terror.

Three hundred feet past the airport fence, the jet dropped from the sky and slammed back to earth. The fuel tanks exploded on impact. Propelled by kinetic energy, the fiery aircraft plowed through the mud, cutting a jagged trough that ceased abruptly in a blot of char where the fuselage disintegrated. From takeoff, the flight lasted four minutes. During those final tortured seconds, nearly a third of the passengers were thrown from the cabin, their bodies hurled against the tall chain link fence along the perimeter of the airfield; the others burned in the explosion and inferno that consumed the plane.

The image on the evening news showed a menacing ball of flame roiling ten stories high, just shy of a tidy apartment complex that housed several dozen elderly residents. Even the anchorman who was trained to report catastrophes with practiced objectivity was stunned into silence at the sight of the disaster. The crash that killed my mother was the worst accident in U.S. aviation history.

My father was in his campus office finalizing the schedule for a departmental conference when the phone rang.

He assumed the hotel rep was calling with quotes for the conference package he'd been negotiating. But the caller was a man from the airline. At first, my father was confused. Personal travel arrangements were the responsibility of the individual attendees. He hadn't reached out to anyone for information on airfares and such.

"Harry Weldon?" the man asked.

"This is he." I can hear my father's crisp, no-nonsense response.

"You are the husband of Sherry Weldon?"

Before my father answered the question, before the caller uttered another word, my dad already knew what the man was going to say.

Listening as the disembodied voice strode delicately yet intently to its awful conclusion, he went cold and began spinning out of control.

"You are completely sure? There is no chance of error?" He remembered remaining calm, but suspects he was probably shouting.

The airline spokesman communicated a controlled sympathy.

Then, following protocol, he began to recite a litany of instructions.

"Do you understand?"

I imagine my father nodding, as if the caller could see him.

"Sir?"

Replaying the scene in my adult mind, I heard my effusive father choke out the one-word response.

"Yes."

Then I saw him drop the receiver into the phone cradle and bury his face in his hands. Later he confided to me that the only thing worse than the pain in his heart was knowing that he had to tell me that my mother was dead.

My father was a careful driver. That afternoon, under force of habit, he obeyed the speed limit and traffic lights as he followed the familiar route across town to Spencer Elementary. After he told the principal, Mrs. Lester, what had happened, they walked together to Room 104. But Mrs. Lester knocked and came in alone. We weren't surprised to see her because she occasionally dropped in on classes "just to check things out," she said. On those rare visits, she was smiling and animated. This was different. The principal who slipped through the door was pale and solemn. Avoiding our unabashed stares, she strode up to Miss Graham, whispered something, and then said I was to come with her.

Me? What had I done? What was going on?

I stood, and the scrape of my chair broke the silence. Uncertain about what I was supposed to do, I began gathering my books.

"It's okay. You can get those later," Miss Graham said as Mrs. Lester crossed the room. Before I could do anything else, the principal took my arm and escorted me to the door.

Something's happened to my father, I thought. But no, he was standing in the hall.

"Are we going to the airport to meet Mom? Is she coming home early?" I asked brightly. Every fiber in my ten-year-old being was determined to deny the bleak reality that I sensed encroaching on my world.

The grim set of my father's mouth and the pain in his eyes frightened me.

I clutched his hand. "What's wrong?" I asked.

He shook his head. Years later, when we talked about the events of that tragic morning, he explained that he'd wanted to tell me immediately, but he had no words.

Usually, my father drove listening to the car radio, but that day we proceeded in silence. As he pulled into the driveway, I started to cry.

He put his arm around me and walked me to the door. In the living room, he dropped onto the couch as if he couldn't go any farther. He tried to pull me down next to him, but I stepped away and remained on my feet.

"What's wrong? What happened? Where's Mom?" I said.

"There's been an accident."

"What happened?" I said again.

Had she changed her mind and packed her swimsuit? I pictured her diving into the pool and hitting her head. Or maybe she slipped in the hotel tub and broke her arm. Or she banged her head when the cab taking her to dinner hit a light pole.

"Mom took an early flight home."

A sick sensation washed over me. I stared at my father. I wanted him to smile and explain that we were on the way to the airport to meet her.

"The plane crashed."

I couldn't comprehend what that meant. I'd flown twice before then and remembered the safety placard in the pouch on the back of the seat in front of me. All those optimistic sketches of people leaning over with their heads in their hands or strapping on safety vests. I pictured my mother sliding down the yellow evacuation chute, barefoot as instructed. Running from the plane, she stumbled and twisted her ankle, so she was hurt, but not badly. She'd wanted to stay and help others who'd been battered in the emergency landing, but the EMTs insisted on taking her to the hospital. How ironic, she said, as they loaded her into the ambulance, that here she was, a doctor who needed other doctors to help her.

As I conjured up these images of hope and rescue, my father continued talking. *No* and *survivors* were among the words he uttered, but the ambulance siren in my head nearly drowned out his voice. Did he say *few* or *some*? I was certain that I'd heard those words as well.

"Where's Mom?"

He was taking much too long to get to what mattered. My question stopped him in mid-sentence. His mouth was slightly agape, open far enough for more words to slip out, but none did. He blinked and pressed his lips together.

He reached out for my hands and spoke the words I didn't want to hear. "Your mother died in the crash."

"No!" I screamed. Wild-eyed, I looked for something to throw, for somewhere to run. But I couldn't move.

My father was on his feet, holding me. He hugged me hard. I pounded my fists on his chest.

"No, no, no." I wrenched loose and crumpled to the floor.

I remember my father kneeling and cradling me in his arms. I remember him crying with me.

"I am so sorry," he said.

I was still weeping when he carried me up to my room. He sat me on the bed and slipped off my shoes, and then he pulled back the covers and tucked me in, nestling my stuffed polar bear in my arms as if I were a small child. I didn't protest. I didn't have the strength, and I didn't know what else to do.

I knew about death. I was the daughter of a doctor, and on rare occasions I heard her tell my father about a patient "who didn't make it." I heard her describe how difficult it was—for her and the nursing staff. I'd had pets that had died.

What I didn't understand was how it could be that I would never see my mother again. The concept did not seem possible. I lay there not moving with these thoughts churning in my head until, at some point, exhausted, my eyes closed, and I slept.

When I woke, the stuffed animal was on the floor next to my bed. The house was silent.

I got up and padded into the hall in my stocking feet. I'd had nothing to eat since breakfast and felt lightheaded, as if I'd been taken apart and reassembled with pieces missing or jumbled back together in the wrong order. Why was I sleeping in the middle of the day? I'd had a nightmare, and I shuddered, remembering the terrifying dream. As I tiptoed down the stairs, I assured myself that everything was okay. My mother was at a medical conference in Florida; she'd be home in the morning. My father was in the kitchen, making dinner. I must have been sick at school and been sent home early. That was it.

The house was dark. The only light came from the streetlamps outside. The living room was deserted, the kitchen empty. In the thin stream of moonlight that filtered in from the yard, I made my way to the den where I found my father slumped in the green and gold-patterned wing chair. His head hung down toward his chest. An empty bottle lay on the floor. An empty glass sat on the table at his elbow.

When I touched his arm, he jolted upright. His eyes were vacant. Looking at him, I knew that the nightmare was real.

"Shouldn't we say a prayer for Mom?" I asked, putting my hand on his.

"Mom?" my father murmured.

"Do you want to pray with me?"

He started to say something and then stopped. When I was older, he told me that he'd wanted to laugh at the suggestion. He'd wanted to taunt me and ask: Pray to whom? To the loving god who inflicts pain and suffering on the innocent? He'd wanted to hurl his question at the world at large but knew I was the only one who would hear it and that his sarcasm would slice my heart. When at last he'd contained his rage, he spoke.

"No," he said. "But you go ahead."

His tone was so weary, so sad, that I wished he had gotten angry.

I went upstairs and knelt by my bed. With my hands pressed together in supplication, I tried to pray, but I didn't know what to say. Dear God, please send my mother back? Dear God, please be good to my mom? Dear God, please, help me!

Somehow, my father and I got through the remainder of the evening and the night. The next morning, I got up early, but my father was already waiting in the kitchen. To set an example for me, he made coffee and ate a piece of toast while I stabbed my spoon into a bowl of cereal.

Around ten, Toby and her parents came over. Her mother, Stacey, embraced my father and me. Her father, Peter, shook hands with my dad and made a rough try at a hug. Toby and I did the same. Neither of us knew what to do or say. While the adults talked, we slipped outside and sat on the patio shivering in the mix of warm sun and cool air.

"You're not at school," I said, to break the awkward silence.

"My mom's taking me later. I mean, when we leave." She pulled at a loose thread on the sleeve of her sweater. "Do you want me to bring any of your books?"

I shrugged. "I don't think so."

"What are you going to do?"

"I don't know."

"You're not going to move, are you?" she said, her voice laced with alarm.

"Move?" The thought hadn't occurred to me. Were we supposed to move? Where would we go? Is that what you did when your mother died? "I don't think so. Not yet anyway."

"I hope you don't. Not ever."

"Me, too," I said. The prospect loomed large and scary.

We stared at the three pumpkins. Toby's family had already carved theirs, but ours would stay untouched and be left to rot.

"I'm really sorry," she said.

I stared at the ground. I knew I was supposed to say "thank you," and I tried. But when I opened my mouth, no words came out.

I wanted Toby to stay, but I was also relieved when her parents came outside and said that it was time for her to go to school. Toby squeezed my hand. Mr. Peters patted my shoulder. Stacey kissed the top of my head, and when she hugged me for the second time that morning, I clung to her. I wanted to hold on forever.

As the day passed, people trickled in. Professors from the college who knew my father. Two doctors from the ER and six nurses, my mother's colleagues from the hospital. Neighbors from up and down the street, as well as others from farther away. Some of the parents of the kids from my class. Miss Graham and Mr. Maier. Even Mrs. Lester.

After the first half dozen visitors, I couldn't stand listening to the litany of sympathies and ran upstairs for the mute comfort that my pet gerbil provided. But I left the door open, with the irrational hope that someone would show up with good news; someone would walk in and say, "Hey, this is all wrong—there's been a mistake."

But no one did.

Our visitors followed the same script. *So sorry. Anything we can do. Please, call.* Many of them brought food or flowers. Finally, the house was quiet. I put Rain back in her cage and slipped out into the hall. On the stairs, I almost gagged at the sweet, obnoxious smell drifting up from the first floor. The aroma intensified as I neared the dining room. Nearly dizzy, I stood in the doorway and stared at the blanket of blossoms that covered the table and sideboard and the bouquets that lined the floor in front of the French doors.

My father was in the kitchen, sitting on a stool before an array of fruit pies, cakes, and platters of cookies and brownies. I must have startled him because he slid off his perch and spun around so quickly, he nearly lost his balance. His eyes were hollow, his gaze unfocused, and he looked at me as if he didn't know who I was. I froze, but the moment passed, and before I could say anything, his arms encircled my shoulders, and he lowered his head to rest on mine. We stayed together that way for a long time. When he straightened up, he brushed the hair from my face.

"You must be hungry," he said.

I shook my head.

He motioned toward the bounty on the counters. “You don’t want anything?”

“A glass of milk,” I said.

I opened the refrigerator, but I couldn’t find the bottle behind the casseroles and bowls of stew and soup that were stuffed onto the shelves. Rather than touch any of it, I closed the door.

A few moments later, Stacey Peters knocked at the door. She brought a plate of ham sandwiches, something simple and approachable, and set it on the small table by the window. While my father and I pretended to eat, she busied herself organizing the rest of the food, putting things into the freezer or pantry, as needed. When she finished in the kitchen, she arranged clusters of flowers throughout the house. Each time I walked past a bouquet, I shut my eyes. To me, flowers were no longer things of beauty. They had become symbols of death.

Several days later, my father flew to Florida to retrieve my mother’s remains. That’s the term that adults used to describe the body of a deceased person, but in this case the word was sadly accurate, because there wasn’t an intact body to bring back, only pieces—the remains of what had been my mother.

Before my father left, I heard Mr. Peters tell him that the airline would take care of the arrangements. “Why punish yourself like this? You don’t have to go down there.”

“Yes, I do. I won’t rest until I’ve met with the county medical examiner. I need him to give me a copy of the official report that identified Sherry's remains. I have to make sure there's no margin for error."

Mr. Peters was quiet for a moment. Then very softly he said, "There were no survivors, Harry."

"That doesn't matter." Then it was my father's turn to be silent. When he spoke, his voice was husky. "I need to see where it happened. You understand that, don't you?"

Mr. Peters didn't say anything, but I'm sure he understood and shook my father's hand.

After my father returned, we held a funeral for my mother. She was given a grand send-off. I'm sure that most of the people who attended the service came because they'd been touched by her in life and wanted to honor her memory. But the outreach was also likely intended to show support for my father and me and to help us through the ordeal. I should have been grateful, but the truth is that I hardly remembered anything about that span of time. Just small bits and pieces.

Like Stacey taking me shopping for a dress. In those days, shopping malls hadn't sprung into existence; if we wanted to buy clothes or shoes, we went to the department store downtown or to the local dry goods store. Mrs. Peters opted for the big store, I think, in part to spare me the sad smiles and glances she knew I'd get from the local shop where everyone knew us.

"Any special color you'd prefer?" she asked as we took in the dress rack in the girls' section.

I had a vague notion that you were supposed to wear black for a funeral, but all I could think of was the forest green sheath my mother had worn at the party.

"Does it matter?" I asked.

"No."

"Then I want green," I said.

Mrs. Peters was an efficient shopper. While I looked on, she sorted through the display, pulling first one garment and then another off the rack and draping them over her arm until she had four dresses for me to try on in the narrow, brightly lit dressing room.

I hated them all. But I knew I had to pick one out, so I settled for the dress I hated the least. It was a deep green color, with a round white collar and a slight flair at the hem. Mrs. Peters called it a "chemise." I had no idea what that meant.

"Do you need shoes?" she asked.

I shook my head. Earlier that fall, my mother had bought me a pair of black patent leather Mary Janes for the concert. I would go to my mother's funeral wearing the shoes she had picked out for me.

The church service was a blur. It wasn't until years later that I realized how remarkable it was that there'd been a service at all. Everything about the ceremony was the antithesis of what my father stood for then, and he must have loathed every aspect of it. So why agree to a religious funeral? For the sake of my mother's memory, surely, and for what he perceived as my emotional needs as well.

My mother and I worshipped at the modest community church at the other end of our block. It was nondenominational, with a sanctuary that could barely hold two hundred people. Many more crowded in for her funeral. They crammed into the pews and stood shoulder to shoulder along the side aisles and the rear wall. I don't remember anything the minister said. While he talked and prayed, I stared at the wooden casket and tried to imagine my mother inside. But I couldn't. One of the doctors from the hospital came forward and talked about my mother. Then Stacey and a teacher from school did the same, but I was deaf to their words of praise.

Sitting there, nothing seemed real except the grip of my father's hand.

He'd taken hold of mine as we left the house, and he held on to it as we walked along the sidewalk to the church, up the concrete stairs, and down the center aisle to the first pew, which was reserved for us. There was no other family. Both my parents were only children, and both their parents were deceased. In the crowded church, we were alone, father and daughter, our own island of misery.

I remember that feeling of being connected to my father and separated from everyone else, and I remember that Mr. Maier stood beside the lectern and played for my mother. The music buffeted the church with haunting melancholy and followed us as we processed out, my father still gripping my hand as we trailed behind the coffin and emerged into the sun.

I shut my eyes to the beauty of the day. I wanted rain and wind and dark clouds to match the way I felt. I wanted the world to end. I wanted to die and be with my mother. I wanted her to push away the cover of the coffin and sit up and smile at me. I wanted everything I could not have.

I hated the ride to the cemetery. I hated walking up the slope of green grass and standing at the edge of the hole that was waiting for us. I hated the thought of my mother being covered with dirt and swallowed by the earth.

I hated everything except that my father still held my hand.

He hadn't cried at church. He didn't cry at the graveside as the minister said those last few words. Even the mournful dirge of "Amazing Grace" played by a troupe of bagpipers left him untouched.

I'd been numb since the start of the ceremony, but in the heavy silence that fell when the last notes of the song faded, I grew agitated and yanked free of my father's grasp. Barely able to breathe, I lurched forward to the coffin and tapped lightly on the lid. Once. Twice.

"Goodbye, Momma," I whispered.

My father made a sound like a sob and stepped up behind me. He put one hand on my shoulder and the other on the coffin. For one final moment, the three of us were connected again. Then he pulled me away, and together we looked on as the bits and pieces that had been collected together and labeled *Sherry Weldon* were lowered into the ground.

What came after was a blur. More food and more people in the house. Toby's parents seemed to be in charge. Mr. Peters poured drinks for those who wanted them. Stacey served food—more food had somehow appeared that morning. During a lull, she fixed plates for me and Toby and told us we could go up to my room if we wanted. We fed Rain and played checkers, but I couldn't concentrate, and Toby eventually got tired of winning. We ended up sitting on the floor and reading. What we didn't do was talk.

Toby was skittish. Once or twice she tried to tell me about something that had happened at school that week, but when I didn't respond, she bit her lip and let it drop. I think my mother's death frightened her. She probably didn't understand it any more than I did. I think I frightened her, too, because now I was different. I was the friend, the girl next door, whose mother had died. I was the one whom people looked at and said "poor thing" about. I wondered how long it would be before we could be easy and comfortable with each other again. In the meantime, I was glad for the books and stories that kept us occupied.

Eventually, the level of noise from downstairs started dropping off. The front door opened and closed. People were leaving. Then the door closed for the last time. In the silence, Stacey called her daughter to go home. Normally, Toby would protest and ask to stay longer, but that afternoon she slammed her book shut and scrambled to her feet. Her eagerness to leave embarrassed us both.

"See you," she said, pausing in the doorway.

"Sure. Bye." I didn't bother to get up.

"Georgia?"

"Yeah?"

"Sorry."

Head down, I nodded.

I don't remember anything else until later when my father came to tuck me in. He had whiskey on his breath. I wanted him to leave. I wanted him to stay. I didn't know what I wanted.

He perched on the edge of the bed and brushed the hair off my forehead. "It's going to be all right," he said. "We'll be okay."

I wanted to believe him, but he looked so sad, I was sure he didn't believe what he was saying either.

"Why did Mom have to die?"

He shook his head. "I don't know. No one knows. Some things in life can't be explained."

"You said science could explain everything."

He tried to smile. "I was wrong."

"It's not fair," I said.

"No, it's not. And if I could change it, I would." He kissed my forehead. "Your mother loved you very much, never forget that."

"I won't."

He kissed my head again. "Get some sleep now."

"Okay."

I couldn't sleep. Neither could he because I heard him go back downstairs. For a while, I listened, trying to imagine what he was doing. But then the house grew silent. Perhaps like me, he was trying to get accustomed to the emptiness.

Exhausted, I lay on my bed and stared up at the dark ceiling. What had happened to my mother? I wondered. Where was she? Could she see me? Was she a ghost who would return to haunt me? I wanted desperately to believe that my mother hadn't been erased, that she lived somewhere in the afterlife, but there was no proof, was there? She herself had said as much. What if my father was right? There was life, there was death, and after that, there was nothing. If that were true, then my mother was lost to me forever. But that didn't seem possible either. Shivering, I curled into a ball and tried to imagine life without her.

After a while, I heard a familiar thud on the stairs, the squeak of the second step from the top. I heard my father stop outside my door and then continue down the hall. I heard the soft click of the door as it closed on the room that used to be theirs and now was his.

I waited until I was sure he was asleep, then I slipped from my bed and tiptoed downstairs. I expected everything to be different, but the house remained unchanged. The living room draperies had been left open, and the shafts of cold moonlight that cascaded through the unfettered windows revealed everything still in place. I wandered from one room to another, ignoring the bouquets, looking for a sign from my mother. Looking for something that would help me understand what death meant or would tell me what the future would bring. The house gave up nothing but the lingering scent of the flowers that had been sent in her honor. I inhaled the rich aroma of roses and lilies of the valley and gagged.

As I passed the den, I noticed the blinking red light on the answering machine. In the crush of events, neither my father nor I had thought to check for messages. I went up to the recorder and, without thinking, I reached out and hit the play button. The message tape whirred. There was a momentary pause, and then the replay function kicked in.

"Hi! I'm on my way home."

My mother's bright voice emerged from the cacophony of airport noise. She paused for a PA announcement. "See you soon."

Then she tapped her wedding ring against the receiver. Once. Twice. "Love you both," she said.

I screamed and the line went dead.

In the end, my father and I were left alone. We tried to cope, but neither of us knew how.

At first, we pretended that life would continue as it always had. One evening, several days after the funeral, my father set the patio table for two and fired up the grill. Watching him flip the cheeseburgers, the one food he'd mastered, I remembered the many times we'd shared this kind of casual meal with my mother. We ate in the dimming light and did fine for a bit. As I nibbled the last of the potato chips, my father drank a beer and told me a story about one of his students. He said it was a funny story, but he didn't laugh, and I didn't either. After a while, I stopped listening to the words tumbling from his mouth. My cheeks were wet. I was crying.

My father wrapped his arm around me. "I miss her too," he said.

I leaned into his shoulder and stared at the spot where my mother should have been sitting. He was looking at it too. We must have remained like that, mute and unmoving, for a long time, because the air suddenly felt cold.

I shivered, and my father hugged me tighter. With his free hand he picked up the empty beer can and crushed it. "We're going to be fine. You're strong. You'll be okay. You'll see."

I didn't believe him.

Without my mother, the house was empty. The world was empty. Life made no sense. Death erased all meaning and purpose. Why should I bother eating or getting up or going to school? My father said that I was strong, but that wasn't true. He wasn't strong either. Without my mother, we were both fragile. I cried. A lot. He drank. A lot.

When our stabs at normalcy failed, he became convinced that the best coping mechanism was to forget as quickly and as much as possible and started blotting my mother's image from the house. One day, he removed every photograph that she was in. Overnight, the walls of the den and the upstairs hallways, which had held the richness of our family history, were stripped of their memories. Two days later, he pulled her books off the dining room shelves.

He thought he was doing the right thing. I wandered through the house like a stranger, too numb to protest.

Everything changed the day I found him packing away her clothes. We'd been let out of school early because of a problem with the plumbing, and Mrs. Peters drove me home with Toby. When I walked in the front door, I saw my father standing near the sofa. He was holding my mother's green dress by the shoulders and swaying gently from side to side, as if my mother were in front of him and they were dancing.

"What are you doing?" I demanded.

He turned and slowly drew his hands in, bringing the shoulders of the dress together. As I watched, he slipped one arm beneath the sheath at the waist and let the top cascade down over it.

"I'm donating your mother's things to charity. She would want them put to good use," he said.

"You can't do that." Didn't he realize that Mom was just on vacation and would need her things when she came home? I reached for the dress, but he lifted it even higher.

I lunged again and again, but he held the dress away from me.

"You can't do this. I won't let you."

"I have to. It's better this way. You'll see," he said.

What I saw then was the horror he had created. My mother's skirts and dresses laid out over the back of the couch. Her sweaters piled on one chair and her blouses on another. Pants, shoes, boots, jackets, coats, scarves, all neatly organized. A stack of empty cardboard boxes by the fireplace waiting to be filled.

I kicked the coffee table, and my mother's pearl necklace skittered to the floor.

"Stop that." My father spoke low and hard.

"You should be dead, not Mom," I said.

He blanched and staggered toward me. He was talking, but I didn't hear anything he said. I couldn't take my eyes off the dress that hung over his arm. Without thinking, I lurched forward and grabbed it.

"Georgia!" He called my name again as I ran from the room and up the stairs.

I flung myself onto my bed and wept. I hated my father. I hated that he didn't sit and cry and gnash his teeth. I hated that he had organized my mother's clothes in neat piles and wasn't sitting on the floor with them heaped in his lap, weeping into the fabric. I hated him because I thought he was trying to forget her.

Other times I hated my mother too—for dying, for leaving me. *Why did you go to that stupid conference? Why didn't you stay home, here with us? With me?* To punish her for deserting me, I stopped cleaning my room and brushing my hair. I handed my homework in late or didn't do it at all. I stopped participating in my classes, refusing to raise my hand even when I knew the answer to the question being asked. I left tests unfinished and hid in the library during recess.

Bedtime was the worst. Every night my father came in and read to me. I couldn't wait for him to leave. When he did, I'd pull the green dress from the back of the closet and slip it over my head. Then I'd cradle Rain to my face and let her lick my tear-streaked cheeks dry.

I realized that I was being cruel to my father. I needed him desperately, but I didn't know how to explain or apologize for my behavior. Neither did he.

Friday night, after we'd finished eating, I put the Scrabble board on the table and then set a martini glass on the sideboard for him. I wanted to make up for the things I'd said earlier that week and thought he would be pleased. He stared at the glass for a long time, then red-faced, he stood and hurled it across the room into the French doors that led to the patio.

Trembling, I pressed against the wall.

For a while, my father stared at the mess he'd made. When he spoke, his voice was tight and eerily subdued.

"Your mother is dead. What we had before, we will not have again." He looked straight at me. "Do you understand?"

I clutched my elbows and rocked on my heels.

"Do you understand?" He repeated the question, his pitch rising.

I mumbled the response he expected from me and then backed out through the doorway.

The next night we watched TV in the den. My father nursed a fat tumbler of vodka. I sat holding a bowl of melting ice cream and stared unseeing at a rerun of *I Love Lucy* on the screen.

That weekend, I heard Mrs. Peters talking to my father in the kitchen. I couldn't make out what she was saying, but the way she spoke sounded urgent and important.

For several minutes, Stacey went on in that jittery way she had when she was excited or nervous. Then a chair scraped hard against the floor. "I know what I'm doing," my father said. I imagined him standing up and leaning toward her, resting both hands flat on the table. "And I'll thank you not to meddle."

The wall clock ticked. Then the kitchen door slammed. From my window, I saw Stacey stumble down the white stone walkway that connected our yards. I waited until she was inside before I went down.

"Who was that?" I asked.

"No one." At the counter my father poured a cup of coffee, his back to me.

"I heard you talking to someone," I said, looking at the strands of hair that curled over his collar.

It was just my imagination, my father said. When he turned around, the bright morning sun illuminated the ridges in his forehead and the cross-hatched lines around his eyes. He forced a smile. "You always had a good imagination."

Like Mom, I wanted to say but didn't.

By the end of October, I was practically living at Toby's house. Life was easier that way, and I don't think my father minded, although that hurt, too. On school days, Toby and I would do our homework together and then work on puzzles or watch TV. On sunny weekends, we rode our bikes, and when it drizzled, we baked chocolate chip cookies. Most evenings, I ate with the Peters family too. I didn't really want to be there amid the forced cheerfulness that I knew was for my benefit, but I dreaded going home even more. People had stopped bringing covered dishes, and often my father forgot to cook. On the nights that I was home, he'd make a quick peanut butter and jelly sandwich for me or open a can of ravioli to heat up on the stove. While I ate, he'd sit and watch, usually without saying anything.

As soon as I'd finished, he'd push his chair away from the table and get up. He'd stand there for a moment, looking in my direction but not seeing me, his eyes piercing through the glass pane above my head, searching for something outside, something that wasn't me. Then he'd turn, and in a familiar ritual, he'd open the cabinet and pull a glass from the top shelf. I'd close my eyes because I didn't need to see what was coming next. I followed his movements by the sounds. The soft sucking burp of the refrigerator door being opened, followed by the *thwack* of the freezer door. The rattle of the ice cube tray in the sink. Then . . . *plink*, as the first sliver of ice skittered into the glass followed by two more in quick succession. *Plink, plink*. By the time I slid from my chair, my father's glass was full of vodka. His plans for the evening had been decided.

People were kind. The neighbors. Teachers. But their lives went on. I was surrounded by people who went through their day-to-day activities as if nothing had changed, because for them nothing had. But for me, everything had changed. I was changed. And the way I was treated changed as well. To the adults, I became an object of pity. To many of my classmates, I became the girl to avoid. Even my friends didn't know what to say, so it became easier for them to say nothing. I was the pariah, the motherless child who trailed a cloud of sadness in her wake that was powerful enough to silence the earth.

I was marked by death. I knew that I was different. Mostly I was angry. I felt cheated and ached for the world as I had known it before. My desire to belong—to be normal again—prompted me to ask Mr. Maier if I would still be able to play in the state competition, fearing that there was an unwritten rule that a student musician without a mother wasn't allowed to participate.

He seemed to find it difficult to respond.

"But, of course, my dear," he said finally in a sad, gentle voice.

Music became my lifeline. At home, I woke up early and practiced alone in my room. After school I went next door and played with Toby. Of the two of us, she had the greater share of talent. Toby was a borderline virtuoso. What I struggled to learn came easily to her.

Inspired by her example, I redoubled my efforts. At school, I attended every rehearsal. I even spent the half hour of morning recess in the music room working on my technique.

"You all have the right notes. Now you must learn to feel, to understand, to become the essence of the music," Ludwig Maier told the class at practice one afternoon. One by one, we played the opening notes of Beethoven's masterpiece.

When my turn came, I drew the bow across the upper string.

"That's it. Once again. Deeper."

I repeated the movement in the other direction.

"Bow."

I grimaced and corrected the movement.

"Good."

A rustle went through the ensemble. *Good* was high praise from Mr. Maier.

"Technically much better. Now from the heart, please," he said.

We'd all heard this earnest command many times. Toby and the rest of the players giggled, but I remained poker-faced.

"From the heart," the old maestro urged again.

My heart was stone, but to please Mr. Maier, I played the best I could. I knew my efforts weren't good enough, not for him. Still, for the precious few seconds that I forgot myself and surrendered to the instrument in my hands, I felt the sadness ease, and I was able to breathe.

In those moments, music became my escape from pain. Again and again, music carried me past the brink of raw sorrow. It was dirge . . . and hope bound together.

On the Tuesday of Thanksgiving week, a chartered bus pulled up outside Spencer Elementary, and I clambered aboard with the rest of the school orchestra. Under a pale blue sky, we headed off to the state competition. Our instruments and neatly packed suitcases were meticulously arranged in the vehicle's undercarriage baggage area. Ever the solicitous mother hen, Ludwig Maier settled into the front seat beneath the two leather satchels that he'd slid onto the overhead rack. One bag held sheet music for the concert. The other contained three giant boxes of chocolates, treats for his students. Stacey and another mother rode across from him, serving as official chaperones.

Toby and I sat together in the middle of the bus. We'd played rock paper scissors to see who got the window seat for the first half of the four-hour drive, and I'd won. We were all giddy with anticipation. Mr. Maier insisted that we had a good chance of winning a top prize, and we believed him, but more important was the trip itself, the exhilaration of leaving behind the routine and the familiar. There was something exciting about the complete separation from school and parents, the night spent in the exotic confines of a big hotel, and a hint of adventure, of acting grown up. For most of us, this was our first taste of freedom.

My nose pressed to the glass, I cheerfully waved to my father. Mingled with my overall elation was the subconscious realization that, for the first time since my mother's death, I was escaping the crushing landscape of grief that had become the backdrop to my life. On the bus, I felt no different from the other kids. We shared a common mission. Our camaraderie and purpose were linked to the man in the front seat and the instruments that bounced ever so gently beneath us.

For the next thirty-six hours, I could forget the plane crash and my mother's funeral and live in the moment.

We were the second of ten orchestras to perform. An unenviable position to be in. And the auditorium? We'd only ever played in our school gym and once in the theater of the local library. The university auditorium was ten times the size of the two of them put together.

When it was our turn to take the stage, I clutched my violin and followed Toby across the polished oak floor. I was so nervous I almost forgot to breathe. Even Toby stumbled a little. When we reached our seats, we both dropped down hard. At school, Mr. Maier was always at the podium when we came in for practice. But there was no one at the podium. No one stood between us and the audience. We had no place to look but at the hundreds of people who were looking at us. I tried to find my father, but in the jumble of faces I could only tell the young from the old. He'd promised! Had something happened to him? Then a man near the center aisle stood up and lifted his hand to wave.

Toby grinned at me. "Look, there's your father," she said.

My dad? That man wasn't my father. My father stood tall. He

was big. His hair was brown. This worn-out, gray-headed man with the stooped shoulders wasn't my father. I blinked. It was him. How had I not noticed what grief had done to him?

Just then, the stage door opened, and the entire audience rose to its feet. The orchestra stood up too as Mr. Maier strode out on the stage. At the podium, he turned and bowed to us. Then he turned to the audience and lifted his baton. Everyone sat, and a curtain of silence fell on the hall.

"The music you are about to hear has special meaning to all of us on the stage," Mr. Maier said. "We are deeply honored to play what many consider the most majestic composition of Ludwig van Beethoven. We approach this concert with humility and pride. But we also appear before you with a great sense of sadness and loss. It is for that reason that we dedicate our performance this lovely day to the memory of Doctor Sherry Weldon, whom we miss very much." He paused and cleared his throat. "May you hear us wherever you are, *mein Liebchen*."

Stacey and the others who knew Sherry rose and applauded. My father stood and raised his arms into the air. First his right and then his left. Holding his hands above his head, he pumped one fist and then the other, using my mother's signal to say he loved me.

As the cheers faded, the maestro pivoted away from the audience. Facing us, he smiled and held his baton high.

Our moment of truth had come.

I took a deep breath, tucked my violin under my chin, and

raised my bow. It was then, at that moment, that I felt a warm, soft touch on my brow. Like the kiss of a feather or a wisp of summer air.

I gasped. *Momma?*

My mother was here. She'd remembered her promise! After her death, she was reaching out to me, just as she said she would. *If it is possible, I will do it. If it is impossible, I will at least try.*

Then, suddenly the baton dropped and I had to play.

B-B-C-D-D-C-B-A-G-G-A-B-B-A-A.

Steeped in sorrow, I played on the wings of joy. We all did. Before us, Mr. Maier swayed and dipped and drew us forward. Led by our beloved maestro, we played from the heart.

As the closing notes echoed through the hall, applause filled the air. The audience rose with shouts of "bravo" and "bravi." Toby reached over and squeezed my knee. Swiping at his right eye, the maestro bowed to the audience. Then he motioned for us to stand. Dumbfounded, we grinned and bowed and bowed again. Mr. Maier enjoyed two curtain calls, and then the stage no longer belonged to us.

We were moving down a narrow rear hallway when, out of nowhere, my father appeared, brandishing a bouquet of bright yellow jonquils.

"You were magnificent. You were all magnificent. I don't care what the judges decide; you were the best," he said, kneeling before me.

I blinked away my tears.

"I know, I know," he whispered as he wrapped his arms around me. "I do too."

Three more orchestras performed that morning and five in the afternoon. They were good, Mr. Maier assured us, but none played to our level. "Your performance was magnificent. You played from the heart. As if Beethoven himself had conducted, not I."

We believed him! We believed him through a lunch of cheeseburgers and milkshakes, but as the hours went by, doubt seeped in, and I began to suspect that our teacher was wrapping us in praise to cushion our ultimate disappointment.

But once again he was right. We were awarded first place.

We were the youngest and the least experienced musicians, and yet we had garnered top honors. There was a trophy, of course, and a half dozen official photos taken on stage, followed by hundreds of images saved for posterity on the box cameras clutched in the hands of our jubilant parents. There were so many moms among them that I slipped away and hid in the bathroom to cry.

By the time the celebration quieted down and we tumbled onto the bus for the ride home, dusk loomed, camouflage for the dark ridge of clouds that bloomed on the horizon.

We'd barely pulled away from the performance hall when the old maestro opened the first gigantic box of candy. As the chocolates made their way down the aisle, I stood up and squeezed next to Toby, ready to grab my share of the treats.

We were miles from the city and climbing a steep and crazily curved stretch of highway when the storm struck. The narrow mountain road afforded no place to pull over and no way to turn back. As sheets of blinding rain cut visibility to near zero, the driver bent over the huge black steering wheel and struggled against the buffeting winds, but we were oblivious to the turmoil until the first crash of thunder drowned out our shouts and loud, happy chatter. A bolt of lightning flashed nearby, and I jolted upright, sending the half-empty box of candy bouncing off my lap into the aisle. Overhead, a cacophony of hail beat on the metal roof.

Stacey stumbled to our seat. She pulled Toby to her lap and wrapped her arm around me.

Mr. Maier followed in her footsteps, determinedly brandishing the second box of chocolates and lurching from one foot to the other as the bus slid around a sudden, sharp curve.

"Sing," he urged us.

I looked at him as if he were speaking Greek.

"Sing," he commanded.

From the rear of the bus, one of the older girls began the opening lines to "Kumbaya," and I meekly joined in.

"Louder!"

I sang with gusto as one by one, more voices picked up the refrain.

At the top of the next rise, the bus emerged into a zone of calm. The winds dropped off, and the drumming rain subsided into a fine drizzle. We stopped singing and cheered. The driver gave a backhanded wave as his shoulders sagged in relief. He had outrun the storm.

Anxious to make up for lost time, he pressed his foot to the gas pedal. But he had miscalculated. Instead of running east, away from the deluge, the road zigzagged to the west, through a series of deep ravines already lashed by the rain.

Despite his speed, the driver safely negotiated the first three turns, but then the bus swept around a hairpin curve and hit a stretch of oil-slick pavement. As the front wheels skidded across the center lane, the rear of the carriage fishtailed onto the narrow shoulder. The sudden maneuver hurtled me headlong toward the window and spun Stacey and Toby into the aisle. I grabbed the back of the seat in front of me and tried to rivet my feet to the floor. Then the rear wheels slid around on the wet pavement, and the front of the bus whipped in the opposite direction and started to slip sideways, off the road.

The driver lost control of the steering wheel.

"Hang on," he yelled, too late.

The speeding vehicle splintered the wooden safety railing and plunged into a deep gorge.

Fueled by momentum, the carriage tore through a forest of spindly pines and ragged underbrush, sowing seeds of glass and metal in its wake. Unable to hold on to the seat or to grasp Mrs.

Peters' outstretched hand, I slammed back and forth against the hard, unforgiving surfaces. Halfway down the slope, the bus flipped on its side. Riding a slalom course of rain-slicked pine needles, the battered hulk ricocheted into a field of gray boulders, gaining speed until it collided with a rock wall, spun around one last time, and shuddered to a halt. At some point in the torturous descent, the glass pane next to me dislodged, and with the abrupt stop, I was flung through the gaping hole.

In the rain-soaked forest, metal creaked and groaned. A weak headlight sent a crooked, yellow grin through the trees. For a moment, the only sound was the sickening whir of the upended tires spinning in the dark abyss, and the only sensation I felt was the river of warm blood oozing from the deep cut in my leg.

Then the wailing began.

PART THREE

Light

I lay in the dirt and dreamed that I was flying. I gasped for air and dreamed that I was dying. I dreamed that I was cold. I dreamed my mother's voice. I dreamed the gentle, sure touch of her surgeon's hands, and then I dreamed that I was warm again.

I opened my eyes and watched my hand float up toward her face.

"Georgia . . ."

As my fingertips brushed her cheek, a tsunami of weeping swept through the forest and swallowed the rest of what she was saying. But I read the sweet affection in her gaze.

"Momma," I said. I had so much more that I wanted to say. *I love you. I miss you.*

At that moment, the brambles behind us parted, and Ludwig Maier staggered out.

The maestro was ghostly pale. His jacket was torn at the shoulder. His trousers were shredded at the knees. His forehead and hands were bloodied. Staggering toward us, he held his arms open wide.

"*Liebchen*," he said and collapsed into my mother's embrace.

The storm had moved beyond the mountains by the time an over-the-road truck driver spotted the smashed guardrail at the top of the rise and phoned the state police. The call came in just as the desk sergeant fielded a report about a missing bus carrying a load of children. Twenty minutes later, a parade of police cars and emergency vehicles wailed onto the winding road that led into the national forest.

The rescuers arrived at the accident scene in a burst of bright light and noisy activity. A group of workers threw up temporary roadblocks while the rescue team slipped and slid down the steep incline. They found the bus first and then made their way to where Mr. Maier lay prostrate on the ground several feet from me. I opened my eyes again to a large woman and a small man kneeling alongside me, their faces ripe with fatigue and angst. While the man felt my limbs for broken bones, the woman checked my vital signs. When she gasped, I knew she had discovered the injury.

"What the . . ." she said.

I tried to smile. I wanted them to know that I was okay. I tried to explain that my mother had come to save me, but the man's loud voice drowned out my words.

"Just clean it. Cover it," he said, and seconds later I felt the sting of the antiseptic.

"You're gonna be fine, sweetheart," the woman said as she draped a pillow of gauze over my wound.

The bus driver was dead at the scene. Ludwig Maier and I, the only two passengers thrown from the vehicle, were the most severely injured. The rescue squad carried the maestro away first. Then they transported me through the trees to a small clearing behind the crumpled bus. Amid the chaos, I drifted in and out of consciousness, waiting my turn to be lifted up above the trees. After what seemed an interminable amount of time, the wind came up and with it the *thwack* of the helicopter blades hacking a path through the darkness. There were shouts and hurried movements. My eyes were masked against the blinding white light that beamed down from the belly of the chopper. The wind chilled my cheeks as the ground dropped away, and I rose up through the narrow canyon between the trees whose menacing branches snatched at the cables that fastened the gurney to the underside of the aircraft. I waited for one of the lifelines to snap. I waited to die.

But the cables held, and when we reached the top of the ridge, I was put into an ambulance. As the vehicle rushed to the University Medical Center, some forty-two miles down the mountain, I was transfused with fresh blood. Some of this I remember; most of this I was told later.

My time in the hospital melted into a haze of sleep and half-heard whispers. I was the miracle child. Afterward, I learned that the description had as much to do with my survival as with the way I presented to the surgeon in the operating room on the night of the crash.

I was the patient the physician couldn't explain. I learned this during one of my lucid periods when I lay with my eyes closed, trying to recall what had happened, and the surgeon and my father talked nearby.

"I was not the first person to treat your daughter," the doctor said. "When I operated on Georgia, I found the ends of the severed artery had already been spliced and sutured together." He told my father that there was no rational explanation for my survival. The bus driver's watch had stopped at 6:13 p.m. The truck driver's call came in a half hour later, and then it took the rescue squad another forty-five minutes to reach the scene. He said that given my injuries, I would have bled out in the interim.

"I knew your wife. I was familiar with her work," the doctor went on. "I cooperated in her research. It was her technique."

"One of the paramedics?"

"No. None of them were qualified to administer that level of treatment."

"Then whoever acted was out of bounds legally, medically. They're not going to admit to such a thing."

"Once the rescue team arrived, no one was alone with your daughter."

There was a pause, unusual for my father. I imagined him

scrubbing his head, thinking. "Those hills are filled with crazies. Someone got there before the rescue squad. An old Army vet holed up in the backwoods, someone trained in medics, someone who knew a technique that was similar to Sherry's."

He went on—angry, defensive. "You had multiple trauma victims here that night. You were understaffed because of the holiday. You thought you saw something familiar."

No. I struggled to speak, but I couldn't push my voice through the BiPAP mask that covered my mouth and nose. *No. Mom did it. Mom saved my life.*

The surgeon sighed. "As you wish," he said quietly. "But the night of the crash, someone saved Georgia from bleeding to death—and it wasn't me."

The door closed. I must have stirred.

"Honey, can you hear me?"

I opened my eyes to my father's stubbled chin and inhaled his cigar-tainted breath. The walls behind him were white, the same color as the tube leading to my arm.

"I saw Mom," I whispered.

He stroked my hair. "I'm sure you thought you did." His voice was thick, his face pale, and his eyes heavy with fatigue and worry.

"She wore a cloak."

"Your mother didn't own a cloak." He spoke quietly but matter-of-factly as if that settled the matter.

"She's so beautiful."

"Yes, she was."

"No. More beautiful than ever."

He took my hand in his. "Georgia . . ."

"She helped me," I said.

"Your mother always helped you." My father bent closer and pressed his lips to my forehead. "Be still now, sweetheart. You need to rest."

Later, when he spoke with the nurse in the hall, he told her that I was hallucinating from the pain medication.

Five days after the accident, I was discharged from the hospital. The nurse helped me change into fresh clothes that my father brought from home. Then she helped me into a wheelchair and handed me a blue plastic bag. "Your other things," she said. I held the bag in my lap as my father wheeled me to the exit.

Outside, he tossed the plastic bag into the trunk and ushered me into the passenger seat. Beneath a sky layered with thick gray clouds, we drove home. It was the Sunday after Thanksgiving, and all along Main Street colorful pictures of turkeys and cornucopias filled the store windows. There were no decorations at our house. The air inside was closed in, stale.

My father tucked a checkered throw around my legs and settled me on the sofa. Then he made a fire. As he worked, I reclined against a cloud of pillows and looked through the doorway into the dining room. My gaze reached the window and the barren landscape outside. The patio furniture had been cleared away, the oak had shed its leaves, and the hill was little more than a rise of dead, brown grass. Staring into the emptiness, I fell asleep. When I woke, it was late afternoon, and my father announced that we were going out for dinner.

He chose his favorite restaurant, one we used to frequent as a family. When my mother was alive, we were always seated under a chandelier in the center of the room. That evening my father and I were led to a small table along the side wall. An arrangement of red and gold chrysanthemums sat between us. While my father studied the menu, I scooped up the petals that had fallen off the flowers and dropped them on the floor.

We began the meal with a Shirley Temple with extra cherries for me and a double vodka martini for my dad.

"To us. We have much for which to be thankful," he said as he clinked his glass against mine.

Like what? I wanted to ask. In the foolish depths of my young heart, I thought he was being callous. Only years later did I realize that his bravado was a façade offered up for my benefit.

The next morning, after breakfast, my father went out for groceries, and I went up to feed Rain. While she nibbled at a dish of pumpkin seeds, I sat on the bed and told her about the concert and the accident. I told her about my mother, too, and it was almost as if she paused in awe and wonder. I was telling her about being in the hospital when I remembered that the doctor had said I should try and walk a little more every day. By then

Rain had finished eating, so I picked her up and held her close as I walked back and forth in the hall. When she started to fidget, I put her back in her cage and went downstairs and walked around the first floor.

On my second circuit, I went as far back as the laundry room at the rear of the house. For some reason, I opened the door. Until then, I'd forgotten about the plastic bag from the hospital, but there it was, shoved in the corner. Without thinking, I opened it. The first thing I pulled out was a small plastic bag with the blood-stained skirt and blouse that I'd worn for the concert. I threw that to the floor. I never wanted to see those clothes again. The next was another small bag with the stuffed zebra and the two books that Mrs. Peters had brought for me. I set those on the washing machine. Oddly, the satchel still wasn't empty.

Curious, I reached deep inside. As I touched the mound of fabric at the bottom, a shiver went up both my arms. Even without looking, I knew that it was my mother's cloak.

Trembling and dizzy, I pulled the garment from the bag. "Oh, Momma," I said.

I don't know how long I stood there clutching the cloak to my chest, remembering how she had folded it into a thick square and placed it underneath my head for a pillow, when I heard a car pull into the driveway. My father was back. I had to hide the cloak. Without thinking, I rolled it into a ball and limped upstairs. While he put away the groceries, I pulled the covers off my bed, draped the cloak over the mattress, and remade the bed.

That night, while Rain rattled in her cage, I fell asleep swaddled in my mother's cloak. When I woke, it was to darkness and silence, darkness deeper than I'd ever imagined and silence so immense it hurt. I wasn't in my bed. I wasn't even in my room. I was sitting upright on a rough, frigid surface with my legs stretched out in front of me and my back pressed against a cold wall. My wound no longer hurt, but my arms and legs were stiff, and my lungs felt leaden inside my chest. I was frightened, but my fear was overshadowed by wonder. Where was I? What was happening?

A deafening scream, like the roar of a thousand tornadoes, shattered the silence. Then a sliver of light slashed the darkness. In that quick flash, I glimpsed my surroundings.

I was in a cave.

Silence again. Darkness again. I waited. In the distance, a thin neon white line emerged. As it raced toward me, the line morphed into a giant ball, and the sharp light softened into a gentle glow. Instantly, the cave was dimly lit.

I looked around.

I was not alone.

In the bend of the hollow, a hunched figure cast a shadow against the wall. I rolled onto my knees and crawled toward the amorphous shape. As I approached, the figure took on a human appearance—man or woman, I could not discern. Not until I was nearly upon it did I realize that I knew the cave dweller.

"Oh, Momma," I said, for truly it was she.

But how was it possible that my vibrant mother had been so horribly transformed? A woman battered, diminished. Her eyes sunken and dull. Her face deeply creviced and worn. Her limbs splotched with yellow bruises. Her hair tangled and void of color. Her feet an ugly collage of blisters and festering burns. Her hands scarred and mangled, the flesh torn and charred. These were my mother's strong surgeon hands, and they lay helpless in her lap.

Though fearful that she would collapse under the cloak's gentle weight, I slipped it off my shoulders and draped it around her skeletal frame.

"Where are we?" I asked, too stunned to weep.

She blinked. "I don't know." Her voice was soft, raspy.

"What happened to you?" Even in asking, I realized that in the telling, she would have to relive the events that had brutalized her and brought her to this forsaken place. But I had to know.

"So much . . ."

I waited. When she began, I bent closer to hear.

First, she spoke about the plane crash, the crushing force of the impact, the instantaneous death of the people aboard. At the precise moment that she died, she said, she was swept into a tunnel of bright light and transported through the horrible chaos of the cosmos. "You cannot imagine," she said and shrank further into herself.

"On the other side of the tunnel wall, savage winds screamed; marauding energy forces—forces powerful enough to alternately compress the human form to the size of a dust mote and then stretch nerve fibers to infinity—battled for dominion. In the time it took for a single breath, waves of blistering heat transformed into icy caves and then reversed the cycle."

Throughout the great beyond, pandemonium held sway, but she remained safe inside the tunnel until at journey's end she was released into a place of blissful calm and beauty.

"The afterlife?" I said.

"*The other.*" She tried to smile. "The place people dream of and wonder about. The ancient Greeks called it the Elysian Plain, but it has been known by many other names as well—heaven, devachan, paradise."

In *the other*, my mother was given her best self. She was reunited with her parents and introduced to her sister who had died at birth. She was introduced to beings from distant arenas of creation, some who spoke a language common to all and some who communicated through a form of mental telepathy. When she was told that she was allowed one visit to Earth and that she could choose the day of her return, my mother chose the day of the concert.

"You were with me on the stage!"

I took her hand and was there with her again, reexperiencing the events as she had. The music, the bus ride, the crash. Everything that had happened was happening again. I saw myself thrown through the broken window and landing unconscious under the trees, my face badly cut and my legs twisted at an odd angle. The ugly gash sliced diagonally across the top of my right thigh. I felt the pain and the warm blood soaking through my skirt and into the ground.

I watched my mother reach toward the open wound and went with her as she was transported back in memory to the ER, to the night the lights went out in the middle of the operation on the young victim of a car accident. She, just a resident, held the severed artery closed with her fingers, waiting and wishing she could do more until, in the confusion of rushing feet and frantic voices, a technician found the switch for the emergency generator, and the lights came on again, and the operating nurse handed her a Potts clamp. The wound she had encountered that night was similar to mine.

As she leaned over me in the woods, her years of training and discipline squelched her fear and emotion. Her ethereal state provided her with hypersensitive touch and vision that could penetrate the dark. The damaged blood vessel was the femoral artery, the primary transport mechanism to the lower extremity.

The nature of the wound was in her favor. My artery was not cleanly cut but torn, nearly shredded at the ends. By touch, my mother located the ragged edges of my ruptured artery. With her physician's touch, she separated the filaments of the arterial wall and spliced them together across the gap, weaving the ragged edges together in a neat seam. I watched incredulously as the warmth from her fingertips cauterized the fine tissue. With each successful lash, the connection strengthened, and the hemorrhagic flow eased. When she finished, she closed the loose flap of flesh over the wound, placed her warm hand over the injury, and waited. She could do no more.

Our eyes locked. "You saved my life."

"Yes."

I told her what the surgeon at the hospital had said and how my father didn't believe him. "He didn't believe me either. He said I was hallucinating."

A sad smile cracked the corners of her parched lips. "It went against his nature. He simply could not."

"But why are you here in this awful place?"

"The guide who accompanied me to Earth was unable to escort me back," she said.

"Why?"

"It doesn't matter."

"Of course, it does." I spoke without knowing where the words came from. With a flash of insight that surpassed my childish capabilities, I realized that my mother's exile was the unbearable price she had to pay for her actions. "Human contact was not allowed during your visit to Earth, was it?" I said.

My mother bowed her head.

"When you saved me from dying, you disobeyed the rule. You relinquished your place in *the other*. You sacrificed an eternity of joy—for me."

A single tear slipped down her striated cheek. "You are my daughter. The love of my heart," she said, lifting her eyes to meet mine. "I would give up anything for you."

"You must return."

"I cannot."

"You must!"

"It has never been done." Again, the hint of a sad smile tugged at her mouth. "I tried."

"Tell me," I said.

With great effort, my mother lifted a gnarled hand and fluttered her fingers in front of my face.

"Watch," she said.

With that, the journey began. I traveled with her as she left the scene of the accident and hopscotched from Earth to the moon, and then past the planets to the outer edge of the solar system. Behind her, Earth was a pinprick of blue in a sprawling ebony sea. Before her, the constellations of the twelve zodiac signs sparkled like a neon bracelet displayed on a cushion of black velvet.

All were dwarfed by the vast expanse of the Milky Way. The center of the galaxy bulged with glorious light, while the fringe of the great discus unfolded into a long, fine layer of starlit, icy ribbon that curved through the heavens. Errant comets and meteors smashed through the galactic structure at dizzying speed, like wild children caught up in an anarchistic game of tag.

Beyond the spectacle, unimaginable multitudes of white micro-spots of light glistened in an endless span of darkness.

My mother knew the grandeur was deceptive. She had made the journey before. Even safe within the white tunnel, she had been aware of the diabolical forces that raged outside its protective walls. This time she was on her own. At her side, I listened as she plotted her strategy to find her way back to her new home.

"I didn't let myself think in terms of size and distance. I would be logical and investigate one quadrant of space at a time. I couldn't fathom the time needed to complete the journey. I was sure that if I kept a level head, I would succeed."

As tongues of brittle cold nipped at her feet and a vicious, unfettered wind screamed past, she plunged into the space.

She didn't stand a chance.

Within Earth's galaxy, a strong gravitational force had protected her from the deadly energy fields that crisscrossed Milton's glassy sea. Once she stepped forward, the system, the universe swallowed her whole.

In a nanosecond, my mother hurtled half a million light-years through the void. The speed was unfathomable and cruel. Connective throat tissue separated from its moorings, aborting her scream. Her ribs snapped. Her ankle and finger joints fused. Her heart and stomach distended and then comingled. Her eyes were wrenched into the hard frame of her skull.

I closed my eyes against the horror.

"Watch," she said again.

And so I did.

I watched as, in unspeakable anguish, she slammed into a galaxy incredibly larger and more grand than the Milky Way. The whirling star cluster fed her into a sea of explosive supernovas. Her skin was charred by blistering white heat, her lungs seared by plumes of putrid gas, her throat coated with hot, suffocating dust.

She tried to turn around but could only plod forward through the flaming center of the chaotic world and then on to the icy outer rim on the far side. Shocked by the contrast between heat and cold, she plunged over the edge into the abyss.

As she plummeted into the ether, a second random field of rays nabbed her. Cyclonic winds blew her across a cavernous black maw that led to a smaller, quieter collection of stars and planets. An oasis, a reprieve? Gulping a gritty, air-like substance, my mother moved on cautiously. Breathing grew more difficult. To navigate the increasingly dense atmosphere, she stroked her arms forward as if she were a swimmer propelling through weighted water. The atmospheric soup thickened to sludge; her velocity slowed sharply. One more small step forward, and she was unable to move.

The galaxy was a trap. My mother stood frozen in place and felt the force of the translucent walls slowly closing in around her.

"What appeared to be empty space was the center core of black matter," she said.

I remember my father telling me about this mysterious mix of invisible, icy subatomic particles that neither gave off, reflected, nor absorbed light.

"I pounded the walls as hard as I could, but the cold had turned my blood viscous, and my movements had slowed and weakened. I was being crushed and sucked into the bottomless pit, sinking, as if into quicksand."

"But you escaped!"

"I did."

"How?"

"I willed myself free."

The cloak had slipped off my mother's shoulder. I pulled it into place. I knew very little of physics, but what she was saying did not seem possible. "I don't understand."

"I had no choice, you see. Physically, I was powerless to save myself; my body could not withstand the force of the black hole. My mind was the one thing I had that the black matter could not affect. It was my only advantage. I stopped struggling and focused all of my thoughts into a single concept, a pinpoint of mental energy that I hoped would be strong enough to withstand the force pressing on me. I came very close to failing. The ugly end of my existence wavered overhead like a shadow. I was about to give up when I pricked the wall. With that one tiny puncture, I disabled the force and was jettisoned out of the void and spun into free space."

"You were safe?"

My mother shook her head. She was snatched up by another stream of imposing energy fields and carried from one punishing galaxy to another. In escaping the black hole, she had traded one horror for another. Too many to count or remember.

Suffering became her life.

When my mother could bear no more, a cosmic free fall dropped her onto a slow-moving asteroid. Her strength vanquished, she curled into a ball and slept. When she woke, she found herself on the very edge of the asteroid. Before her, the rugged surface sloped down to oblivion, but behind, it tilted upward to a great jagged height. She clawed up the towering fin of rock and found herself on a large plain rimmed by a stone wall pockmarked with caves. She crawled to the largest of the hollows and collapsed.

From the relative safety of the asteroid, she surveyed the endless chasm of space. On Earth, she had gazed up into the heavens and wondered at the grandeur of the celestial world. But no more. Her Earth had vanished into memory.

"Earth!" A bitter sob rose in my mother's throat as she uttered the word.

In *the other*, she had met inhabitants from a thousand worlds, but in the great yawning expanse that she had traversed, she'd seen no sign of organic life. Only one deadly galaxy after another, each raging with greater brutality than the one before. The splendor of creation mocked her memory, filling her with dread, horror, and humility.

"I tried to overcome the force of the universe, and I failed. The bedlam was impenetrable. The way unnavigable. I could not find my way through. I cannot go on."

"You must. I'll help you," I cried.

"Oh, my dear child," she said. "I fear that is impossible. There is no returning."

"There must be!" I said, reaching toward her.

My hand caressed my mother's cheek once again. I blinked and she vanished.

"Momma!"

I was back in my room, back in my bed. Confused and wild with fear, I scrambled to my feet and peered into the shadows, searching for her.

“Momma, where are you?” I whispered. But I knew where she was. My mother was stranded on a black rock in the unknowable cosmos. I had lost her once to death and again to the endless void that surrounds us.

Or had I? Perhaps the encounter had been a dream, a nightmare.

Desperate for a sign, I pawed at the covers looking for her cloak. It was gone.

Rain rattled her cage, and I began to cry.

Winter’s first hard freeze had struck that night. When I came down to breakfast the next morning, the lawn was white, and the neighboring rooftops shimmered with a thin layer of hoarfrost. At the edge of our patio, a row of shriveled, brown chrysanthemums drooped in their clay pots. A large pumpkin, forgotten from Halloween, had collapsed into itself, leaving the orange flesh mottled with black decay.

My father stood at the stove frying eggs. I poured a glass of milk and set it on the table. Pretending to listen to the radio announcer chatter about the weather, I laid out two paper napkins and then slipped into my chair.

My father remained at the stove, his back to me. “I saw Mom last night,” I said.

He stiffened and a moment passed. “In a dream,” he said. “That will happen.” Offering up a tight smile, he turned and put a plate of fried potatoes and scrambled eggs before me. “I dream about her too," he said, taking his seat.

"You do?" I sat up straight, surprised and encouraged by the soft longing in his voice.

"But this wasn't a dream. Mom is out there," I said, convinced he would understand.

I waved vaguely toward the ceiling and the intergalactic world that lay beyond. "She's lost out there somewhere in space."

My father set his coffee cup down hard, sending brown liquid sloshing over the rim. "Lost? Georgia, your mother isn't lost. She's dead. The plane crashed and everyone on it died."

"Mom is hurt. She needs to find the way back."

"Back? Back where?"

I hesitated and then replied in a whisper. "To *the other*, the place beyond the chaos."

"Oh, Georgia." He reached across the table and grabbed my hand. "Please, honey, don't do this to yourself."

"I should have known that you wouldn't believe me." I barely spat the words out.

He was ashen. "You had a dream, that's all." He spoke softly, but I felt the strength of his conviction in his voice. "There is no *other* out there. No paradise, no heaven, no afterlife. Mom is dead. She's gone."

I yanked free from his grasp. "The gospel according to Dad!" I was on my feet, shouting. "You live, you die—that's it. But what if you're wrong?" I had never spoken to my father this way. Unmoored, I trembled with rage.

"I made Mom promise that when she died, she would try and

contact me, and she did. She was at the concert. When I was on the stage getting ready to play, I felt her alongside me. After the bus crashed, I saw her. She saved my life." Tears trickled down my cheeks as I spoke.

"I saw her again last night. She's alone and lost and in horrible pain." I started to raise my hands as my mother had done, somehow imagining that if I could show him what she had shown me, then he would understand. But, of course, I couldn't do that.

My arms dropped to my sides, and our eyes locked. The force of faith against the power of disbelief.

"Mom is doomed because she helped me. Now I have to help her."

But how? What could I do? My mother had kept her promise. How could I keep mine? I was only ten years old, a mere child.

The next morning, I was on the school bus thinking about my mother marooned in the menacing universe, remembering how frightened she'd been and how despairing it was when she said that she couldn't find her way through the bedlam. That's when I realized that what she needed was a path to follow, the same as Hansel and Gretel, who had followed a line of breadcrumbs through the forest to reach safety. My mother had taught me to pray. Now I would pray for her, and, indeed, if there were miracles, then my childish supplications would rise up through the heavens and leave a celestial trail that would lead her through the labyrinth and back to *the other.*

As the bus rambled past the light poles wound with red and white striped Christmas ribbons, I huddled with Toby and told her everything.

"Your mother is stranded on an asteroid?"

"Yeah, I guess, or a rocky planet. It doesn't matter."

"You're sure this wasn't a dream?"

"No, remember, I told you the cloak is gone. Will you help?"

Toby bit her lip and then nodded yes. "When? Where?"

Until then, I didn't have a plan. "Tonight," I said. "We'll go to the top of the hill. The closer we are to the stars when we pray, the better."

Toby nodded again. "But how will we know if our prayers are working?"

I leaned against the seatback and turned toward the window. "My mother will send us a sign," I said, with the absolute conviction of a child.

It was already dark by the time I finished my homework and ate dinner. I told my father that I'd borrowed a book from Toby and asked if I could return it. He was in the den, reading, with a glass of whiskey on the table. Of course, he said. Quickly, I slipped into my gray wool coat and went outside.

Toby waited behind the oak tree, her purple knit hat pulled low over her ears. "I told my parents I was coming over to watch TV with you," she said.

An owl hooted in the distance, and overhead, thick clouds

rolled across the sky, dimming the faint light of the crescent moon and the few visible stars. As soon as we were out of the yard, I reached into my pocket for my flashlight. Though I expected more from it than the pencil ray of light that struggled to penetrate the darkness that enveloped us, I reassured Toby that I could do this blindfolded. Shoulder to shoulder, so close I could hear her anxious breathing, we plodded over the uneven ground. By the time we reached the summit, our shoes were wet and our pants damp to the knees.

Toby shivered and shoved her hands into the pockets of her thin jacket. "I wish I'd worn gloves," she murmured.

I wished I'd worn a hat, but said nothing.

I turned off the light just as the clouds thickened further and the night closed in on us.

Toby grabbed my arm. "I can't see anything," she said.

"You'll get used to it." I tried to sound brave. "Stand still and wait."

"It's spooky."

Below, the warm, comforting lights of home and town winked and beckoned us to come down out of the cold and wind. It would have been so easy to give up, but I couldn't. I thought of my mother and began to pray. Toby joined in.

We said all the prayers we knew, and then we made up our own. The wind quickened and swept another layer of clouds over us. Rain misted on our heads as we pleaded for my mother to be saved, our voices small against the great shroud of silence on the hill.

Then, in the distance, we heard voices. Stacey and my father were calling to us. Anxious, alarmed.

"Georgia! Toby! Girls, where are you?"

I ignored them. Toby tugged at my sleeve. "We've got to go. We've been out too long."

I shrugged her off.

Toby pulled at my arm again. "Please. We're gonna get in trouble." She hesitated. "We'll try again. I promise."

There was another round of shouts from the base of the hill.

"We're here," Toby called out.

Cold and numb, we stumbled down the slope. My father scowled. Stacey pulled us close.

"I thought the two of you were inside watching TV. What were you doing up there?" she said.

"Nothing," we said in unison.

Heavy sleet was falling the next evening when Toby came for dinner. There'd be no going outside.

As I draped her wet jacket over the back of a chair, she glanced toward the living room. "Where's your Christmas tree?" she asked innocently.

Before I could say anything, my father answered. His tone was sharp, professorial. "We are a secular household. We don't observe Christmas."

I looked at him. "We used to, and Mom loved to decorate the tree," I said quietly.

"Yes, she did," my father sputtered. Then he marched us into the kitchen. "Hot dogs okay?" he asked too loudly.

He turned on the burners, and we roasted the wieners on forks over the flames while he poured potato chips into a blue bowl. While we ate, he nursed a glass of vodka and told stories about his first job working as a soda jerk.

"The worst was when I squirted whipping cream in a woman's face. She had a little boy, about three, with her. He started laughing, and then I did too, and she only got more upset. Want to see?"

My father was already on his feet heading to the refrigerator. He pulled out a can of whipping cream and brandished it wildly around the table, pretending to douse us in white foam. We laughed politely, but the joke was already worn thin. Abruptly he set the red and white can on the counter next to the bottle of vodka.

Toby squirmed and studied her empty plate. I saw my father's arm lift and pour.

"You haven't eaten, Daddy," I said.

"I'll get something later." He pushed the bottle toward the wall. "Why don't you girls go amuse yourselves?"

We scrambled up the stairs to my room. I closed the door and jumped on the bed, scattering my pile of stuffed animals and sending several pillows over the edge.

Toby sat cross-legged on the floor. "Is he always like that? Now, I mean?" she asked.

"Yeah. Sort of."

"Too bad." She fluffed a pillow and tossed it up to me. "Have you dreamt about your mother again?"

"It wasn't a dream."

"I know. But have you seen her again?"

I shook my head.

Toby waited a moment and then spoke again. "What are we going to do?"

"Keep praying," I said.

Kneeling side by side at the bed, we bowed our heads and prayed silently. Then we sat next to each other by the window, tucked our knees under our chins, and murmured our entreaties out loud while Rain spun in her cage.

The weather kept us inside the rest of the week. We prayed together every night, but nothing happened. I sensed Toby's enthusiasm waning, and though my resolve remained strong, I was forced to admit that my idea wasn't working. I had to find another way to rescue my mother.

Ironically, my father, a man who only believed in what he could see or touch, a man who refused to believe that I had witnessed my mother in her desperate straits, was the one who showed me how I could help her.

He did so unwittingly, of course.

On the Sunday after the incident in the kitchen, I came downstairs to find him in the dining room with his coffee and the morning paper. Across from him on the table sat a black leather violin case. He'd replaced my violin, which had been destroyed in the crash.

I stood in the doorway, unable to prod myself closer.

"For you," he said.

Since the concert, I hadn't thought about playing again. A substitute music teacher had been hired to fill in for Mr. Maier, who was still in the hospital, but I hadn't attended class or gone to orchestra practice. The school owned a small collection of instruments that we were allowed to use as needed, so access to a violin wasn't the problem. The problem was me. I didn't want to play. I couldn't imagine my palm caressing the neck, my fingers pressing on the strings, my jaw on the chin rest, and the bow at the ready in my other hand.

"Dad . . ." I pictured the red velour lining inside the case and the shine and soft curves of the instrument that lay against it and tried to tell him that I didn't want the new violin, that I couldn't play and would never play again, but the words dried in my mouth.

"Go on, open it," he said, nodding toward the case. A faint smile played across his lips, and a flicker of something other than the despair that I had come to accept as permanent flashed in his eyes.

Not wanting to disappoint him, I walked up to the table and ran my hands over the case. My heart fluttered, and before I fully realized what I was doing, I was holding the violin and playing the familiar notes of the "Ode to Joy."

Appalled, I stopped.

“What’s wrong? You don’t like the violin?” my father asked.

I shook my head. “No. It’s perfect.”

“Go on then,” he said.

I flung the instrument onto the table.

My father started. “Georgia, what is it? I told the luthier that I wanted a violin similar to your other one. Is there something wrong with it?”

I almost laughed. The violin was exquisite, and I hated it. I hated it because I couldn’t play, because playing that piece broke my heart.

We had supper in the kitchen that evening. I don’t remember what we ate or what little we said. Since my mother’s death, our meals had been tinged with sorrow, but that was the saddest one yet.

Afterwards, I went into the dining room where my new violin lay on the table exactly as I’d left it that morning. I knew it was expensive and that my father meant well. To try and make amends for my behavior earlier, I carried the instrument to my room. Once there, I shoved it under the bed.

That night, as I had done every night for the past weeks, I curled into myself on the bed. I was a child bitterly aware of the challenge I’d undertaken and of my inability to fulfill it. Because of my failings, my mother was doomed to spend eternity in agony.

Downstairs, the hall clock chimed the passing hours. As I stared toward the ceiling, I counted the gentle tones. Ten. Eleven.

Twelve. I must have fallen asleep eventually because the next thing I knew, a ribbon of pale light was filtering in along the edge of the curtains. I slid from bed, smiling. The solution had come to me in my sleep. I knew what to do. Kneeling on the floor, I hummed the music I had been unable to play the previous day and reached underneath for the violin.

Would Toby help me? I was first on the bus that Monday morning. Waiting for my friend, I stared out the window and bit my lip. As usual, Toby was late. When she finally appeared, I grabbed her arm and yanked her down to the seat.

"What?" she said, trying to pull away.

I held on and leaned closer. "The 'Ode to Joy.' The world's greatest prayer," I whispered.

She looked at me, puzzled. Then her eyes grew bright, and I knew that she understood.

"Words alone are too soft. We need to make ourselves heard. We need power and strength. We need music."

Toby grinned. "We need our violins."

We agreed to meet at six that evening. Now I needed a reason to go up the hill in the dark. After school I hid my violin in the garage, and after supper I asked my father if Toby and I could take the telescope to the summit to study the craters on the moon.

Extra credit for science, I explained, and of course, he said yes.

A few minutes later I walked out the door with the telescope. Toby was waiting by the garage. We made the switch and hurried through the yard and up the slope.

The climb kept us warm, but when we reached the top, we were at the mercy of the wind. I shivered inside my jacket. And the gloves that we'd both remembered to wear were useless once we had our instruments in hand.

The sky was clear, but the chilly air dulled the sound, rendering our first attempts weak and tentative.

"Concentrate. Think," I said, as much to myself as to Toby.

In a few minutes the strings went flat. We tuned the violins and kept on. My fingers grew numb. I struggled to navigate my left hand up and down the neck and to hold the bow securely with my right. Every few minutes I glanced up, searching for a small sign that our meager efforts had succeeded.

A stellar sea spread overhead. The specter was beautiful, bewildering, and unyielding.

Please. Please, I silently pleaded.

Nothing happened.

We played even when we couldn't feel the tips of our fingers. We played until Toby lowered her bow. "We have to stop now," she said.

"Until tomorrow?" I said, hopefully.

"Until tomorrow."

After Toby went home, I switched my case for the telescope and went in. My father had hot chocolate waiting.

"Which craters did you find? Copernicus? Petavius? Tycho?" he said, rattling off the names of several lunar basins.

"We had trouble focusing the telescope," I said. "We'll try again tomorrow."

The next day at school, Toby recruited three other players to join us. "They want to help," she said.

I was wary. "What did you tell them?"

"The truth."

"The truth shall set you free," my father always said. He'd embraced the concept for years and had made it the basis of his scientific study, of his life. Which, if you think of it, is very odd because it's a biblical tenet, a quote from John, an exhortation to faith.

I knew better than to argue with Toby, and in fact, I admired her ingenuity.

Once again, I told my father the fiction about studying the moon and then headed to Toby's, where we met, ostensibly, to go caroling. This time we were well bundled against the cold, but instead of wandering down the street bright with Christmas lights, I led the entourage up the dark hill. Though we again struggled to keep our fingers nimble and the strings in tune, the reinforcements made us feel more confident, and our music took on a strong sense of depth and purpose. It was a spectacular, eerie concert, the same piece repeated again and again.

Toby's father heard the music when he took out the trash.

"How was the caroling?" Mrs. Peters asked brightly when we returned to Toby's kitchen.

"Great." Toby and I spoke at once.

"I bet it wasn't as good as your concert on the hill," Mr. Peters said sarcastically. He was about to go on when his wife set a platter of cookies on the table.

"What are you talking about, dear?" Stacey said. "The kids weren't on the hill."

Eyes downcast, we five remained silent.

After the others left, Mr. Peters wrangled the story out of Toby.

"You poor disillusioned child," Stacey said, wrapping me in a suffocating hug. "And you, too," she said to Toby. "Both of you, so well-meaning but . . ." Her voice trailed off. "Peter, don't be angry with them."

But Toby's father was furious. He dismissed the account of my mother at the bus crash and everything that happened afterward as juvenile fantasy. Mostly he was angry with Toby for what he called her complete disregard for the welfare of her violin.

"Do you have any idea how much that violin cost?" He didn't wait for a response. "Well, let me tell you that it cost a lot. In fact, more than a lot. More than we can afford." Cold weather would ruin it, he said. Without his express permission, she was forbidden to remove the instrument from the house.

Once he finished admonishing his daughter, Mr. Peters called my father and relayed the story. Listening to him, I realized how crazy it sounded. Music. Path. Rescue. How could I expect anyone to believe me?

"I hold you responsible for this nonsense," Mr. Peters told my father.

"It's not his fault," I said, but I'd waited too long to speak. Toby's dad had hung up and was already out of the room.

I looked at Toby and then at her mother. "I'm not disillusioned. Ask, Mr. Maier. He'll tell you. He'd help if he knew what we were doing."

Stacey took both my hands in her grasp. "I'm sorry, dear, but your poor teacher was very seriously injured. He's been in a coma since the accident." She hesitated and then went on. "The doctors said he may never recover."

Toby and her mother offered to walk me home, but I shook my head. I had to face my father alone.

He was waiting in the kitchen, and he was even more furious than Mr. Peters.

"What the hell do you think you're doing?" he demanded.

I avoided his hard gaze. "You wouldn't understand," I said. In truth, at that moment, I wasn't even sure that I understood.

"It's about that dream, isn't it?"

The memory of that night flashed before me, and I was transformed. Defiant. All self-doubt vanished. I looked at my father. "It wasn't a dream."

He disregarded my response with a wave of his hand and ranted on. "And dragging Toby into this, and your other friends!

How do you justify that?"

"They wanted to help."

"Help how? Help you create a path for your mother to follow back to *the other*." He spoke with the same sarcastic tone as Toby's father had.

He reached for me, but I stepped away. "Do you honestly believe that Mom is lost and that you have figured out a way to guide her safely through the cosmos to the front door of this imaginary Eden of yours?"

We both knew that the idea seemed absurd, but I would not yield.

"I only did what I believed was right. Isn't that what you always said I should do?"

"This is different." He made a sound of deep frustration and scrubbed his hands over his face. When he spoke again, his manner was soft, deflated. "How'd you come up with that crazy idea anyway?"

"I got it from you."

"What . . . ?"

"That night you took Mom and me up to the hill with the telescope, you talked about magnetic waves that could carry signals from the other planets to Earth. If signals can come down, why can't they go up, too?"

My father stared at me, momentarily speechless.

"You love your mother very deeply," he said, finally.

"Oh yes," I cried.

He held out his arms, and I ran to him. "I miss her so much."

"I know," he said softly as he held me close. "I do, too."

"She needs me," I whispered.

My father stroked my hair and said nothing.

Later, alone in my room, I took a piece of yellow paper from the box of stationery that my mother had given me for my birthday. Sitting on the floor, I wrote a letter to my music teacher:

Dear Mr. Maier,

I am very sorry that you were hurt in the bus crash. Please, get better soon. I need your help.

Sincerely,

Georgia Weldon

The next morning, after I finished my toast and hot chocolate, I walked to the corner and mailed the letter to the hospital, hoping it would reach the maestro, hoping the doctors were wrong. Then I came home to practice my scales. But my violin wasn't in the den.

I turned and found my father standing in the doorway.

"You need a few days off," he said. "The rest will do you good."

I protested, but he wouldn't relent. I ran to Toby's house. Her violin was gone too, hidden by her parents who'd offered up the same weak excuse.

"They're all in it together," Toby said.

We rode our bikes to school to see if the janitor would let us into the music room where the extra instruments were stored. But the building was locked for the holiday, and there was no one around.

Dejected, we sat on the swings in the playground. I debated whether to tell Toby about my letter to Mr. Maier, but I knew how disappointed she was, and after what her mother had said about his chances of recovery, I thought it wasn't fair to get her hopes up.

"We need a plan," Toby said. She pushed off and pumped herself higher.

"I know. We'll think of something." I hunched my shoulders against the cold.

Beside me, Toby skidded to a stop. "I have a recording from the concert," she said. "We could connect a bunch of extension cords to my record player and carry it up the hill."

"And then what?"

She looked at me as if I were dense.

"We'd keep playing the 'Ode to Joy.' We could repeat it a zillion times."

"Wow!"

For a moment she almost had me convinced. Then I shook my head. "We don't have enough extension cords," I said, kicking at the patch of sand beneath the swing. "Besides, we'd probably get electrocuted. And besides that, it just wouldn't be the same. The music has to be real."

We were halfway home when I slammed on my brakes. Behind me, Toby skidded to a stop.

"What—"

I interrupted before she could finish. "Christmas Eve. The community festival. The orchestra can't perform without us, and we can't play without our violins."

"Yes!" Toby's grin quickly faded. "But then how will we get to the hill?"

"I don't know, but I'll figure out a way."

For the next two days I was the perfect docile daughter. I baked cookies and finished a thousand-piece puzzle of the Amazon jungle. I helped Toby wrap her presents and waited as she arranged them under the tree in her living room. I wrapped my father's gift, too, and slid the box under my bed because I didn't know what else to do with it. Beneath the façade, I was desperately trying to come up with a plan to return to the summit.

The evening before the festival, my father and I sat together watching TV. "Are you doing okay?" he asked as he patted my knee.

"I'm fine," I said.

But I wasn't fine. I was tortured by the memory of my suffering mother and my failure to rescue her.

My room was in shadows when I woke on Christmas Eve morning. I was shivering. My quilt was heaped on the floor. I must have kicked it off the bed during the night. I looked down at the coverlet, but I didn't pick it up. I deserved to be cold, I thought, as cold as my mother trapped on that frigid black rock.

Rain rattled in her cage. The wind howled outside. I lay on my back, quivering with each breath.

After a long while, the aroma of fresh coffee wafted up from the kitchen, and my father called to me. He'd made pancakes, but he served them in silence. I didn't care. Wrapped in my robe, I was ashamed of my cowardice but grateful to be warm.

Snow had fallen during the night. I didn't realize it until my father asked me to help shovel.

Toby and her dad were out, too. Mr. Peters and my father barely spoke to each other. When the sidewalks were cleared, they went their separate ways. But Toby and I stayed outside to build a snowman.

"Is your mom still upset?" I said as we started rolling the snow for the base.

"I can't tell. She hasn't said much, and this morning she went to the hospital."

"Is she sick?" I tried not to panic. Toby didn't deserve to lose her mother, too.

"No, she's okay. She went to see a friend, that's all. She said she had an important message to deliver."

By the time we finished our snowman, Stacey still wasn't home.

My father and I ate a late lunch that day. He had little to say to me, and afterward, he got up from the table and walked away. I was clearing up when he returned, carrying my violin.

"You'll need time to tune it," he said, handing me the case.

I wanted to scream at him, but I merely nodded. "Thank you," I said.

The annual city hall holiday concert started at three o'clock, and by two thirty, the great atrium was packed. Thirty minutes later the first performers—a troupe of preschool ballerinas—went on. Toby and I waited in one of the long hallways that extended from the lobby. The others in our small circle looked at me. Their eyes asked the same question: When? But I didn't have a plan.

"I don't know. Soon," I whispered.

We were last in the lineup, and by the time we finished, it was nearly four and already getting dark outside.

I had to come up with something quickly. But how would I get everyone from the venue to the hill?

In one of those ironic moments that life sometimes hands to you, it was my father who provided the solution when he invited the parents to our house for post-performance drinks.

Perhaps he felt a need to inject a bit of cheer into our cheerless house, or he was lonely for adult company. Whether from empathy or the urge for a glass of something stronger than the lemonade served at the event, the parents all accepted. With the parents came the other children, and with them came their violins.

The adults immediately gathered around the sideboard where my father had hastily assembled an informal bar. Once the drinks were poured, there was a toast, followed by another. When our parents were on their third round of drinks, I motioned Toby and the others into the kitchen and then out the door and into the yard.

Free of the house, we raced toward the hill.

"That was easy," Toby said when we reached the halfway point.

I stopped and looked down the slope at my house. "Maybe too easy," I said.

"What do you mean?"

I kicked at the snow. "I mean that my father knows exactly where we are and what we're doing."

"He does?"

"This is part of his plan. He's waiting for us to fail."

"Why? I don't understand."

I started climbing again. "My father always said that we learn best when we learn for ourselves. He doesn't believe anything I've said about my mother. He thinks I'm imagining things and that what we're trying to do is crazy, and that if—when—we fail tonight, I'll have to accept the truth—his truth—that there is nothing after death, and my mother is truly gone forever."

"But he's wrong, isn't he?"

I looked at Toby. For a moment, I didn't know what to say. My sweet, wonderful friend had never had a moment's doubt. Her trust showed in her eyes. I grabbed her arm. "Of course he's wrong. And for my mother's sake, we have to prove it."

The others were waiting for us at the top.

"It's Christmas," I said, lifting my violin from its case. "We must believe."

In the dark and cold, we played. I saw no sign in the dark sky. My fingers grew stiff and frozen, but I refused to stop. Faith made me—made all of us—persist in the face of all futility. Fueled by innocence and idealism, we played on.

Time passed. The cold cramped our arms and stung our feet.

Still, we persisted.

Eventually, of course, our parents came for us. Full of self-righteous indignation, the adults advanced on the hill, corralled their protesting children, and propelled them down the dark, slippery incline and through the now-trampled yard.

My father and I were the last ones down. He carried my violin in one hand and held my wrist with the other. Humiliated, defeated, I stumbled after him. I had fulfilled his prophecy and failed my mother.

The adults milled about the driveway, preparing to leave. Suddenly, amid their smug outpouring of farewells and good wishes, when it seemed all was lost, an avalanche of sound erupted. Stunned, confused, they pivoted toward the hill from whence the haunting, triumphant strains of "Ode to Joy" poured forth. The music was so powerful it sounded as if a dozen musicians had materialized on the starlit slope. But I knew that only one person could play the music in that special way.

"It's the maestro!" I shouted.

The music played on.

I tore free from my father's grip and grabbed my violin. "Mr. Maier is on the hill," I said as I doubled back across the lawn.

Toby rushed toward me, her hat askew and her purple scarf cascading down over her shoulder. "The maestro? You're sure?"

"Yes!" I cried joyfully. I didn't know if my letter had reached him. I didn't know how he had come to be there, but he was on the hill, and that was all that mattered.

Toby turned around toward the yard, shouting, "To the hill!"

The other children picked up the cry and ran after us through the trampled snow.

I reached the old maestro first.

"I got your note," he said and kissed my forehead. "The nurse told me everything, and so here I am."

If my dear Ludwig Maier suffered any residual effects from the accident, if he was weakened from his long hospital stay, there were no indications of impairment in his performance that night. If anything, the venerable musician seemed invigorated, greeting us warmly as we clustered around him. Then he lifted his antique violin to his chin and gave us the look we all recognized from class.

"On my count, we begin," he called. He paused long enough for us to get our instruments out and tune them to his. When we were ready, he continued. "One, two, three."

As we played, the sweet, urgent sound of the "Ode to Joy" rang out into the frosty night air and propelled the simple melody—B-B-C-D-D-C-B-A-G-G-A-B-B-A-A—up toward the stars.

From that moment, there was no compromise in our performance. The tempo was brisk. The music, bold and commanding. The harmonics combined extremes of greatness and sorrow, and yet did so with utter simplicity. The notes exuded an air of noble grace. The melody ascended upward from the hill, carrying our humble offerings of beauty and truth.

Under a bright wintry sky, we melted into the music. With our beloved teacher, we moved as a single body. We felt and thought as a solitary mind. In perfect, desperate union, we played on.

We played from the heart. We played to save my mother.

But even as we reached beyond our best, the universe stared down with blank disregard.

I knew the others were watching me.

"We must keep going," I said.

The wind clawed my cheeks; the cold paralyzed my feet and cramped my arms and hands. My breath crystallized in the air. Still, I played on.

I played on as my father and the other parents swarmed back up the slope. Mumbling. Complaining. Determined to stop us. Enough was enough.

But when the adults crested the summit, their ragtag procession juddered to a momentary halt at the scene before them. Huddled together in a small circle of light, a handful of exhausted, shivering children gathered around a stooped, old man and played music to the gods.

Aware of the entourage of outraged parents, Mr. Maier straightened slightly and called to them over his shoulder. "You were not there. I was. I saw Doctor Sherry—and I play for her, now."

They must have thought him mad. For a few moments, they cast uncertain glances at each other. How could this be? What now?

Mr. Peters took a step toward my father. Stacey tried to stop him, but he ignored her and kept coming. "This can't go on," he said firmly.

At that, my father nodded and plodded across the snow-covered ground toward us.

"For the sake of the children, please, stop," he begged Mr. Maier.

The elderly gentleman shook his head. "For the sake of the children and of what is right, I cannot."

My father moved toward me. "Georgia, my dear child," he said, reaching for my violin.

I spun away and tilted my face up to the northwest. Focused on the dark patch of the night sky above the horizon, I played on.

"Georgia, please. I'm only trying to help you."

"I know," I said.

Blinking back tears, I almost missed the pinprick of light that poked through the curtain of darkness. I gasped, and the speck faded. "Please, please," I whispered. Exhausted and weakened by the cold, I wondered if I had only imagined the flash. But there it was again. The light was minuscule, maybe unreal. I squinted to keep the small bright glimmer in focus. Barely able to breathe, I watched. One second, the mote twinkled. Then it dimmed. "No," I said, reaching up with my bow as if I could touch it, but it was gone. I stared into the dark sky. A moment passed, and I lowered the bow.

"Georgia." My father's voice grew hard.

"No, Dad, no," I said, weeping as I steadied the violin under my chin. Before I could bring the bow to the strings, the light exploded.

"Look." I raised my arm again and pointed to the big, bright, beautiful display in the sky.

"Georgia!" My father kept his eyes pinned on me.

"Look!" I cried again, commanding him to turn his gaze upward. "Look," I shouted to the others.

One by one, the children lowered their violins and lifted their eyes up toward the spectacle unfolding millions of miles away. Only Mr. Maier played on.

As we gazed at the night sky, the bright orb reverberated against the ebony palette of the universe. Streams of brilliant color shot from the center and whirled madly until they coalesced into a rotating river of light that spun into a dazzling halo around the new star.

The mob of parents surged forward. The children cheered. Ludwig Maier played on.

My father dropped to his knees.

Moments later, a second nova erupted. In quick, staccato fashion, the twin stars flared, just as the headlights on my mother's car had the day she talked to my class, just as she'd tapped her wedding ring on the phone. First one and then the other. One. Two.

My father staggered to his feet. With his eyes pinned on the twin stars, he scooped me off the ground.

"Mom's secret signal. *Love you*," I whispered.

"I . . ." he couldn't go on.

"The music worked," I said.

An impossible quest sparked by grief and love had triumphed.

Overhead, the twin stars pulsed again. "Dad, look. Mom is telling us she's okay."

He stared at the sky. "I don't understand."

"You don't have to understand. Like Mom said, all you need to believe is a change of heart."

With tears welling in his eyes, my father smiled.

Together on the windswept slope, his damp cheek pressed to mine, we watched the twin lights flash one last time before they slowly, gently dissolved into the black abyss. In those precious few moments, I felt my mother's presence just as I had in the concert hall. Waves of bittersweet emotion washed over me. My mother had entered another place. She was gone from my life forever, but her suffering had ended, and her long journey was complete.

Safe in my father's arms, I pressed my fingertips to my lips and blew a kiss at the night sky. Then I did it again. My sign back to my mother.

Love you, too, Mom.

EPILOGUE

After the others had left, my father and I drove off in search of a Christmas tree. Day had already faded into night, and the local vendors had all turned off their lights and gone home, leaving a hodgepodge of dark, vacant lots along the snow-covered streets. It didn't seem possible that there wasn't a single tree left for us to buy, but by the time we'd approached the edge of the city, we'd nearly lost hope.

Just as we were about to give up, we turned a corner and spied a dimly lit ragtag lot in the middle of an otherwise dark roadway. A portly man stood in the shadows, hunched inside his jacket and rubbing his hands above a small fire that burned inside a dented metal drum. Behind him, a handful of scraggly firs leaned against a makeshift wooden railing.

"Last-minute shopping, heh?" the man said, as we emerged through a veil of falling snow. He looked old and sounded tired. Before we could answer, he pulled his black watch cap low on his forehead and gestured toward the trees that no one had wanted. "Well, take your pick."

We chose the tallest of the bunch and lashed it to the top of the car with twine. All the way home, I worried that the tree would tumble off into the street, but my father drove with care, and we made it back with it still in place.

Inside our living room the fir looked as scrawny and pathetic as it had on the tree lot. But once watered and warmed, it shook off its tired façade, allowing its branches to fall open into an almost perfect circle and perfuming the air with the sweet aroma of fresh pine. We had a bit of a party that evening, with Toby and her parents helping us decorate the tree while Mr. Maier sat on the sofa and supervised the process.

When we finished, I perched on the arm of the couch. There was something I needed to ask him. "How did your nurse know?" I whispered.

Mr. Maier patted my hand. "She said that someone came to see her that morning and told her everything that had been going on, everything you'd been doing."

"Who?"

The maestro shrugged. He told me that he didn't know, but then he smiled, and as he did so, I could swear that he winked at Mrs. Peters across the room. She stood near the fire holding a cup of eggnog, and I could swear she smiled back as she lifted the drink to her lips.

I stayed up until midnight, sitting by the tree and thinking about my mother and the people who had helped me help her. Later, in my room, I knelt at the window and stared past the hill to the patch of black sky where she had flashed her signal to me. I would never see those two lights again; no one would, for they would never reappear.

To this day, the twin stars that exploded above the slope on that magical Christmas Eve remain an unexplained phenomenon. Government observation stations reported no unusual celestial activity that evening. The automatic recording devices at the local observatory yielded no notable data for the entire twenty-four-hour period. Asked to comment on the transient appearance of the two stars, a cadre of astronomers, meteorologists, and other specialists dismissed the purported sighting as seasonally generated mass hysteria. One expert called it wishful thinking.

Of all those who were on the hill that evening, I am the only one still here. Mr. Maier was the first to leave us; my father was the second. The others followed one by one. For many years, Toby and I were the sole survivors. Eventually she moved away. But every year on Christmas Eve, I'd call her. With the airwaves between us open, we'd tune our violins and play "Ode to Joy," in honor of our maestro, in honor of that evening, and in honor of my mother.

Toby died last winter. Since her passing, I've been the one person who could bear witness to the events of that Christmas Eve, the one person who knows the truth of what happened on the hill behind our house on South Granite Street.

And now, so do you.

ACKNOWLEDGMENTS

StarSong evolved from the question that both my daughters asked when each turned ten: What happens when you die? Both the answer I gave and the promise I made to my children are the same that Sherry Weldon gives her daughter, Georgia, in the story.

In the maelstrom of ideas that followed my discussions with my girls, I was struck by the biblical quote from John 15:13: "No greater love hath someone than they give up their life for another." But what if a mother's love is greater than the love lauded in the gospel? What can a mother give up that is more precious than life itself to save her child? The conclusion I arrived at became the inspiration for *StarSong*.

Like the enormous, glittering universe that surrounds us, the heart contains mysteries we cannot fathom. In the realm of the heart, love is all-powerful. In the world of magical realism, a ten-year-old child can pursue an impossible goal and succeed. Indeed, all our hopes and dreams can come true.

Although the storyline for *StarSong* evolved quickly, the manuscript went through many iterations and often stalled while I focused on my other writing projects before finally reaching this point. Seeing *StarSong* in print is a dream come true, and I owe many thanks to my dear friend Carol Moffat as well as to the many others who generously read and critiqued the story on its long, meandering journey. I am especially grateful to those who did so in this final stage, including Ellen Pinkham, Jenny Milchman, Larry Lundy, Silvia Acevedo, Anna Fallon, Lynne Shaner, and Joyce Burns Zeiss.

Finding a publisher for a novella is a challenge; finding a publisher willing to take on a writer working outside her established genre is even more difficult. In Kristin Mitchell of Little Creek Press, I discovered both. Kristin and the staff at LCP have been exceptional. With them, *StarSong* has found a good home. I hope that the story also finds a home with you, the reader.

ABOUT THE AUTHOR

Patricia Skalka won the Midwest Book Award for Best Thriller/Mystery and the Edna Ferber Fiction Book Award for her Dave Cubiak Door County Mystery series. A board member of the Society of Midland Authors and Teaching Artist at Write On, Door County, she's been named a Notable Wisconsin Author by the Wisconsin State Library Association.

Patricia turned to fiction after a successful career as a Staff Writer for Reader's Digest, a nationally published freelance writer, and a nonfiction author. Her books include *Nurses On Our Own*, the true story of two women who started the first independent nurse practitioner office in the country.

A long-time Chicagoan, Patricia currently lives in Milwaukee.